BEST ROAD YET

BEST ROAD YET

STORIES BY

RYAN STONE

Press 53
Winston-Salem

Press 53, LLC
PO Box 30314
Winston-Salem, NC 27130

First Edition

Cover photo © 2010 by Andrew Kafahl

Cover design by Kevin Morgan Watson

Author photo by Kristin Dallavis

Library of Congress Control Number: 2010936841

Printed on acid-free paper
ISBN: 9781935708087

For my wife

CONTENTS

ACKNOWLEDGMENTS

"Run Nowhere" first appeared in *RE:AL* Vol. 33, Number 1, and received First Prize in Short Story in the 2009 Press 53 Open Awards and was published in the 2009 *Press 53 Open Awards Anthology*.

"Man, Woman, Gun" first appeared in *The South Carolina Review* Volume 41, Number 2

"River Beast" first appeared in *Karamu* Volume 21, Number 2

"Everything Has Its Place" first appeared in *The Madison Review* Volume 27, Number 2

"I Just Found This Hat" first appeared in *Wisconsin Review* Volume 40, Issue 1

"Best Road Yet" first appeared in *Fresh Boiled Peanuts* Issue 3

"Play for Us" in *Big Muddy* Volume 11, Issue 1

"The Same as Everywhere Else" first appeared in *Whiskey Island Magazine* Issue 53

"Scrapping a Bird" first appeared in *Elder Mountain* Issue 1

"Cold Start" first appeared in *Elder Mountain* Issue 2

"Catching Earl" first appeared in *Natural Bridge* Number 19

"Even This Is Silence" first appeared in *The Strange Fruit* Volume 1, Issue 2

BEST
ROAD
YET

Run Nowhere

month before my son was born, I found out about him. Annie, a girl I'd known in Knoxville, called me up and told me she was eight months pregnant, that the boy was mine, that on the sonogram he had all his fingers and toes and a big mouth. Just like her, she laughed. I cried into the phone. The next day, I drove to Knoxville and met Annie in a Super 8 Motel. Her big belly swayed when she walked. I took her out to eat at the Waffle House, and we caught up on old times. She told me she had a boyfriend who worked construction, and she asked me what I did. I didn't tell her the truth.

In the motel room, I rubbed her bare belly as we lay curled up together on the sheets. Her breasts were swollen. She smoked.

"Should you be doing that?" I asked.

"Don't hurt none," she said. "Don't hurt nobody."

We stayed there a long time and watched a Nick Nolte movie in the room. Then we ordered a late dinner from a Chinese delivery place and ate it with the blinds open. The cars sped past on the Interstate. I thought maybe someone would see us.

"I'm supposed to be in Arkansas," she laughed.

I laughed and didn't tell her about my girlfriend back home, about how I'd said I had a sick uncle, and how I knew she didn't believe me.

I kissed Annie the next morning, long and hard in the parking lot, and drove back to Missouri with a cracked feeling in the back of my throat.

In the morning, we mowed grass. Elonzo took the riding mower out to where Hank Seeger, the cemetery superintendent, told him to and mowed and mowed. Earl and I grabbed the weedeaters and went out and clipped the grass short around the headstones where Elonzo couldn't reach with the mower. Heat burned up through our shoes, right out of the grass. There were no trees, except the low pines that outlined the cemetery's borders. Earl stopped, slumped on his weedeater, stared at the sky. The clouds rolled overhead. We waited for Seeger to come out and tell us to take a break. He did. He came lumbering out of the tool-shed, his big body leaning sideways, each step a labor of indifference. Someone had died, so Seeger climbed onto the backhoe. We probably knew the person, but when you work here, when you dig a hole every now and then for a familiar face, you try not to think about it. We sat under a shade tree, smoked, drank some of Elonzo's whiskey-tainted lemonade, and took it easy while Seeger worked the backhoe off somewhere in some other section of the cemetery. We chewed on long brown stems of grass.

"Susan's pregnant," Earl said.

"Yeah?" I asked. It hadn't been long since Earl's son had been killed. We could see where he was buried from where we sat. "Congratulations," I said.

"I think it's a girl."

"How do you know?"

"I've got a strange feeling in my bones about it," he said.

We could hear Seeger revving up the backhoe over the hill. The hydraulics moaned as he tried to dislodge something—a rock, a sarcophagus, an old tombstone long buried.

"You're that sure, huh?"

"I'm sure," he said.

We went back to drinking. Earl reached down and took hold of a grasshopper, pinching its legs together. It began to chew, and brown spit stained Earl's fingers. The backhoe kept at it. A deep and sagging sigh rang out. I could imagine Seeger cussing at the thing's worthlessness. *Worthless piece of shit*, he always said. He said it about equipment. He said it about us, too.

"It's funny," Earl said, "the feelings you get. I get feelings about everything nowadays. Just nothing that seems to matter." He tossed the grasshopper. It opened its wings and sputtered away, the same sound baseball cards made in our bicycle spokes when we were kids, only lower, softer, closer to the earth. "I get little feelings about the way the car is turning, like it's turning too fast, or a feeling about an intersection or a semi behind me. I get the shivers when a car comes up behind us at night. Stuff like that." He sat for a moment. "I get feelings like the life is being squeezed right out of me. That's how I feel when I think of Susan being pregnant again."

"That's no good," I said. I didn't know what to say.

Two hours later, Seeger drove the backhoe over the hill up to where we were and barked at us for lounging around. We went back to work, clipping the grass short again. The grasshoppers boiled up from the grass and scattered from our tromping feet. Their wings beat that soft sputter that we couldn't hear over the weedeater's two-cycle. We could only imagine what they sounded like as they darted away.

We were digging a hole for a spruce tree just above a fresh grave. The flowers, still piled high, stunk in the heat. Elonzo pounded the ground with posthole diggers, pinching out earth as if he were blessed with giant fingers. Earl and I cut through it with our spades and waited for Elonzo to clear the hole.

"It's definitely a girl," Earl said. "I'm so glad it's a girl. If it were another boy, I don't know what I'd do with myself. I couldn't look at another boy."

He leaned down on his spade, his thin arms stretched out. The sun fell on his neck and made him look red.

"You're happy?" I asked.

Elonzo smiled. "Clear hole," he said. We began digging again.

Earl said, "It's Susan I'm worried about. She doesn't know how to take it. It was her idea."

"To have another?"

"To try and have a life," he said.

I didn't tell him about my son, now born, now living with another man and an old girlfriend who I still slept with in small motel rooms along the Interstate in Knoxville. I said, "At least you're making it."

Seeger came out and looked at the hole, pronounced it deep enough even though it wasn't.

"Put the tree in," he said. "Boss called down. We've got to get a site dug in section A-3 for tomorrow. Better go down and inspect the tent. No holes. Could rain."

He got on the backhoe, and the three of us went to the shed and started inspecting the tent for holes. Around the storage shed, mice clawed at the ground. They ran through the dust and into the shed where we could hear them scratching at the tin. We went up and down the splayed-out tent, our eyes digging into the fabric, but we found nothing. So Elonzo took out his pocketknife and cut a rip in the tent's middle, and we spent the afternoon fixing it.

Elonzo and Earl were in the toolshed, hunkered over a table where they studied a triangle peg-jump game. Earl kept trying to help Elonzo understand the mechanics: "Jump over a peg and you get to remove it. Remove all of them but one and you win." He demonstrated a move and took out the little plastic peg with one end pointed like a spear, the other coned like a trumpet, and set it down. It rolled a little on the table, making a hollow sound. Elonzo seemed to be getting it.

"Like this?" he asked. He picked up a peg, jumped over two pegs, and removed them.

"That's a good move," Earl said. "You'd be good at checkers."

"I know checkers," Elonzo said.

Pretty soon they had it figured out and could get the triangle down to one or two pegs every time. Elonzo was happy with himself. That was the nicest thing about having him around. He found enjoyment in simplistic things like finishing a hole or mowing the expansive patch of grass on the cemetery's west side where no one was buried yet. His optimism kept me sharp. It always felt like summer around Elonzo.

Earl said he felt close to Elonzo, who was seventeen, just a little older than his son would have been. Elonzo didn't have any family to speak of, none that we knew of anyway. He lived in an apartment outside the city with ten or twelve other workers. They jumped from job to job, making money under the table. Some days Elonzo wasn't at the cemetery. When he came back, he would tell us how much money he had made putting up road construction signs. We were always surprised at the amount of money and the distance he was willing to travel for it. The furthest he ever went was north Texas for a week, and he worked his way back across Oklahoma. Sometimes I looked at my paycheck. I looked at my girlfriend and our boxy house on the city's south side, and I thought about moving to Knoxville for good, finding a little place that looked completely different, living in motels for a while, anything to snatch the rug out from under myself. I'd have to take Elonzo with me, of course, because otherwise I wouldn't know what to do.

Seeger came in, broke up the peg game, and ordered us out to mow. There was always some place to mow in the cemetery. We went outside. He put Elonzo on the mower and gave trimmers to Earl and me. The sun was dry, hot, and burning. It felt much hotter than it should have been in the morning. I choked the trimmer and pulled the starter three times until it coughed. Then I flipped the switch to Half Choke and pulled again. The trimmer fired up clean and buzzed and choked on air bubbles in the gas line until they cleared; then it was a fine, smooth hum, and I flipped it to Run. Earl stood opposite me, fiddling with his trimmer. He kept looking at the gas tank, a little plastic one on the side. I could see there was plenty of fuel. I stopped my trimmer, and the quiet surprised me.

"What's up?" I asked.

"I don't think this fuel is mixed," he said.

"Looked good to me," I said.

He turned the trimmer over in his hand.

"I better be sure," he said and went back in the shed. I fired up my trimmer. The gas was mixed. I'd filled both from the same can. I headed out to where Seeger wanted us to trim, the sun hot on my forehead, the flies already circling like tiny vultures.

I finished most of the section before I realized Earl hadn't joined me. I put the trimmer down, the vibration still in my arms, and went to the shed. He sat at the table with the peg game in front of him. I went over and pulled up a chair.

"Seeger'll fire you," I said, "if you don't get going."

"I'm trying it backwards," he said. "If I can solve it backwards, I can solve it forwards." He kept taking all the pegs out and putting them back in when he made a move. It gave me a headache, but maybe it was just the sun. He said, "You ever feel like you can't run fast enough to get away?"

I thought of Knoxville, how fast I'd drive when I went there, how fast I'd drive away.

"Sure," I said. I glanced at the door, expecting Seeger, but he didn't come. Maybe he was gone. We could hear Elonzo's mower running over on the west side. He might see my trimmer and wonder what happened.

"I just keep moving," Earl said. "That's all I can do." He picked up one of the pegs and tossed it on the floor. "This would be a lot easier with fewer choices."

We were in a Motel 6. We were always staying in rooms with numbers, hotels with numbers. She was standing at the window. Our son lay asleep in his playpen. He snored in little puffs.

"I told him about us," she said. She stood by the window, watching out into the Knoxville night. The cars flashed by. The only light in the room came from the old television. The colors kept changing, making Annie's face go from blue to red to a greenish gold.

"He knows we're here right now," she said.

"The hotel?" I asked, sitting up. "He knows which hotel?"

"He knows everything," she said. She fumbled around in her purse for something. I thought it was a cigarette, but she brought out a pack of Freedent and popped a piece in her mouth. She tossed her purse on the bed next to me, and I noticed the peppermint smell coming from it.

"I quit," she said, chewing.

"When?"

"After he was born," she said. "I just decided one day in the kitchen to quit. I was lighting the cig with the gas stove, and I thought, this is ridiculous. So I put it in the trash and haven't touched one since."

"That's great," I said. "So how did he take it?" I was fishing. I wanted to know if he would come storming through the door, and I found myself shifting toward the edge of the bed, prepping for a defense.

"He wants to go on *Maury*," she said, giggling. "He thinks he might be his."

"Is that possible?"

"No," she said. "I was pregnant when I met him." She popped her gum. "Just a month or so, but I knew."

There were deep shadows in the room from the overcast sky. It started to rain a little. The drizzle dusted the cars outside.

"I have this guy I work with who is having a daughter," I said. "He's excited about it."

"That's great," she said.

"He's glad it's not a boy. His son died in a car wreck. It was his fault, or so he says, and we work in the cemetery where the boy is buried." It was the first time I'd spoken to her about my job, about Earl. "It's some kind of torture for him, I guess."

"That's awful," she said.

"I think I'd like to be a father," I said. She turned from the window. Behind her I could see the lights out in the parking lot shimmering in the rain. "I mean, look at this," I said. "This isn't a life." We had thrown our clothes around the room in small piles. We hadn't made love. There was less and less of that because the boy didn't sleep much. Now we mostly just watched TV, ordered Chinese food, and watched him toddle around the room, tripping over the piles of clothes.

"That would be nice," Annie said. She came over to the bed. "Do you think you can do better than who I'm with now?"

She looked me up and down, sized me up, seeing me as a guy who cuts grass for a living, a guy who has no horizon, just a stretch of grass that goes and goes and goes until the green makes you crazy. I got up and began packing my stuff. I stuffed it all into my duffel bag and tossed it near the door. She was still on the bed, our son still asleep in his playpen. I went over and looked down at him. He was soft, silent now, no puffs of air, just still and breathing slowly. I hoped he dreamt of something he liked, something that would make him wake up laughing. I hoped it wasn't me.

At the door, I kissed her like I always did because I always left before she did. She had to get the baby ready.

"Nelson'll be here soon," she said.

"Here?"

"I told him I was going to end it."

"Are you?" I asked.

"I don't want to," she said. "I like what you said."

"So do I," I said, and I kissed her again. When I turned around, a Buick Skylark pulled into the parking lot. It slid into a parking spot just beneath our second-floor room. A man got out, a man I can only assume was Nelson. He had broad shoulders, a thick neck, skin dark as well-watered dirt. I don't know if it was him. I just think of him that way, there in the parking lot. All the rain seemed to hit him. When I dream of this moment, the rain only falls on him like in cartoons—a cloud follows him. And I'm dry.

We had to dig the grave by hand. The backhoe broke down. Seeger went to find a replacement part, but all the stores were closed. It was just Elonzo and me down in the hole, the dirt walled around us, black and soft and crumbling down into our shirts. Elonzo didn't say much, just kept working at the ground with the pickaxe. We were about six feet down, and according to cemetery regulations, the top of the coffin had to be six feet under. So we had about three feet to go. With the backhoe, that would be nothing.

We would tear the earth apart in no time, but with picks and shovels, it would take at least several hours working straight through. Earl went home for dinner with his family and said he would be back and would bring some floodlights he had in the garage. Elonzo and I kept at it, banging away at the dirt down in the hole.

I started telling Elonzo about Annie, my son, Nelson, and Knoxville to pass the time. I figured, with his English skills, he could only pick up about half of it. Maybe that was true, and maybe it wasn't. Maybe he only picked up the tone of my voice, the way my face scrunched up when I talked about my son. He was young, Elonzo, just a boy really, but there was something about him that said he knew more than most men. He stopped with the pickaxe and reached up to touch me. He touched my shoulder and clamped down with his hand, his face went straight and strong, his mouth a line. There was dirt in his black hair. With the fading light, I only saw his eyes, the bright whites.

"When I'm in Las Cruces," he said, "I leave father for good." He shook his head. Then he smiled. "Then I come here. Meet you. Meet Mr. Earl. A good thing." He nodded, smiling constantly.

Flashlight beams appeared above us. We thought it was Earl setting up the floodlights, but the beams stayed focused on us, and we quit working. There were men talking a foot above our heads. I could see their shoes. I lifted my head up, called out. The flashlight spots stopped moving around the hole. They centered on our faces.

"There an Elonzo Miguel Rodriguez here?" a voice from behind the flashlight asked. It was just dark enough to conceal the man's face.

"Sure," I said, and Elonzo looked at me. His eyes were calm. He smiled a little.

"You need to come on up." The ladder shook a little. The voice's owner must have kicked it for emphasis.

Elonzo went up first. Caked mud from his boots fell on me. It stuck to the ladder rungs. I followed him up and found him standing with two men in beige uniforms, stars on their chests. They handcuffed Elonzo, and one of the men held him by the left arm.

"What's this?" I asked.

"He's being deported," one said, the man not holding Elonzo's arm. He had a clipboard. "There a Manny Seeger around?"

"He's not here," I said.

He looked back at the clipboard. "How about a Benjamin Wilson?"

"He's the superintendent," I said. "He's not here either. No one's here but us. They've all gone home." I looked over at Elonzo who kept smiling a little. The corners of his mouth turned up just enough to give his eyes a glint in the flashlight beams. Behind him, the sun faded, the clouds a deep red.

"We'll come back tomorrow to see them," he said. "Tell them there'll be a fine. Pretty hefty. This is their third offense."

"What about him?" I asked, pointing to Elonzo. "Can't he stay around and help me finish this hole?"

The man with the clipboard stared at me, narrowed his eyes. "This is serious," he said. And they took Elonzo, one man on each arm, and pulled him away toward a parked car with flashing lights in the window. They put him in the back where the windows were tinted. As he leaned in, he glanced back at me. The sun was nearly gone, but I saw him smile. His teeth white. Nothing but black everywhere, a hole we're dug into, except his teeth. White like the sun.

The fine was bigger than anyone expected, and Ben Wilson called to tell Seeger that he would have to let us go. When Earl came in to work, I told him about the fine. I told him about Elonzo and the car.

"He smiled at me," I said, hoping this made it better.

"Did he say anything about me?" Earl asked. When I told him they had taken Elonzo away, he sat down at the folding table and held his head in his hands. "Did he say to tell me goodbye?"

"Yes," I said. That kid said everything with his smile.

Earl took some pride in that, but he didn't relax. I told him about losing his job, and he leaned forward and said, "I'm not leaving here. Ever."

Seeger came in and told us he had refigured everything and could keep one of us on. He said he would give us the day to talk about it, think it over, and come to him with a decision after work. We went out to the west plot, the one where there were no gravesites, and began working on the grass. My arms ached. I had finished the grave sometime early that morning, and the trimmer felt heavy in my hand. Neither of us got on the mower, but Earl kept stopping, turning off his trimmer, and standing in the sun as if listening for something.

I didn't stop for lunch. I worked straight through, took off early, and went to Seeger's office. I told him I needed the job more than Earl. I told him I couldn't get back on my feet if I lost another job. The whole time I was thinking about Annie in Knoxville, about how Nelson had come for her so willingly, quietly. Like some kind of dignified knight. And every time I thought about that, I went on even more to Seeger.

"I have a son," I said to him. I hadn't told anyone about Annie, except Elonzo. "I need to be able to take care of my son."

I waited in the shed that evening, playing the peg game. I jumped the pegs over each other, and I could never quite figure it out. I would leave four, five pegs on the board. I kept resetting them, trying again. I heard the shouts from Seeger's office and had trouble believing he had seen things my way. But I can be convincing sometimes. I hadn't tried with Annie. Hadn't tried with the men who took Elonzo. But with Seeger, that afternoon, I made a good case. Earl came out of the office. He came to the shed. There was sweat all over his shirt, grass stains on his boots.

"You've killed me," he said. He gathered his things. Outside, I could hear the sound of Seeger firing up the repaired backhoe to dig another grave.

River Beast

I'm making a run south down I-55 to replenish my supply. I have Trent with me. He has a small Swiss Army knife in his front pocket and keeps pulling it out and digging around in his fingernails. Even though I'm driving, I watch him as he digs dirt out, cutting himself a little.

"I got a letter from a bill collector the other day," he says. He's down in debt as low as he can go. If he gets any lower, they'll bury him alive with his shoes on. He goes on, "It's all the time now. I really appreciate this, man. I really, really do. You don't know how much I appreciate this. I owe you big time."

I want him to shut up. I spit in my spit cup.

"Just stay cool, okay? Sammy doesn't like strangers much."

"But you called him right? You called him?"

"Yeah," I say. "I called him."

Trent is nervous about this whole thing. It makes him twitch and move around like he has to piss. He's never bought or sold before; he's never done much of anything before. He takes the pocketknife out and digs at his thumbnail.

"Why don't you put that thing away," I tell him. "And don't get it out when we get to Sammy's."

"It calms me down." He holds the pocketknife up. It's one of those little ones, with a plastic toothpick in the end, but the toothpick is missing. "Besides, it feels good."

"Just put it away."

He slides it into his back pocket.

We are off the Interstate. A few miles back, we stopped at a gas station. Trent took a leak while I gassed up and bought cigarettes, a couple of frosted doughnuts, and a pint of Malibu rum. We eat the doughnuts and drink some of the rum. The mix is nice, sweet and staunch. Trent bites a doughnut and then takes a swig, swishes it around in his mouth.

We met three years ago. He was living in the apartment across from me with his girlfriend. They'd fight and he'd end up in the hallway, sitting with his knees pulled close to his chest until she had calmed down. One time, I let him in my place. After that, he knocked on my door every time. That's why he's here, because he has a door to knock on. She'd show up after a while, and we'd all sit and watch reruns of *The Andy Griffith Show* and smoke. It was weird at first, sitting on the couch with the two of them, not talking, only the sound of blown smoke, Andy, Aunt Bea, and Barney's high wheeze. Weird at first, then fine, then normal. The way most things go. They'd leave after a while, and that was the extent of our relationship: a simple knock and a long sit. Until he told me about his debt, about guys wearing sunglasses coming to his door at night. That only means one or two things. So I told him I'd let him in on the next run, get him a little dough. I'm bad like that, soft as a rotten apple. Of course, he'd have to work for it, but he said he would. Desperate people say such things.

I take the first right after we pass through Wynott. The south side of town looks much different than I remember.

There's a major chain gas station, a small hotel, and a strip mall with a dozen or so shops, including a small Walmart. Sixteen years ago, the land was smooth and flat and dotted with elm tree groves. In the summer, boys hauled hay and chased the same girls over and over. Now, at dusk, I can already see the gas station's artificial light hovering over the highway. It makes me sad, makes me miss my boyhood home, which never really existed, just enough to make it a smidge of a memory. Trent pokes my shoulder.

"Where did you live?" he asks.

"Over there," I say with a wave of my hand toward the water tower's shadow, and we drive on to Sammy's turn off.

It's a gravel road leading down to the river. Before Sammy took it over, Ray Wallace owned it, and I worked for him. I always felt like that part of my life was detached because my best friend had been here, too. He was gone now, somewhere out west, and I hadn't heard from him in years. Me? I keep coming back. It's as if I can't rip myself away from anything I've already sewn up. When I needed money, I came to see Ray about pushing some weed after Ray got into that when he was trying to keep from selling the place. When Ray finally sold it to Sammy, I came to see about whatever it was he had. Normally meth, but sometimes anything. Sometimes painkillers, and I took some of those myself. There are trenches in the road dug by runoff. We used to fill them with shovels and bags of dirt we brought up from the river. Now they are wide like open wounds. We pull up to the resort's general store and get out.

Trent stays by the car, leaning against the door. He has a pack of cigarettes rolled up his sleeve and looks fake. I go up and knock on the screen door, and Sammy comes to it. His eyes are red, and his hair is greasy and bunched on his head like a thicket of thorns.

"Hey," he says and opens the door.

The store isn't stocked except for a few random boxes of

non-perishables. The coolers behind the counter are long
unplugged and smell of rotted earth from when Ray kept
Styrofoam containers filled with worms and dirt. He'd pack
his weed in those coolers, too. Behind the worms. Said it
kept the stuff fresh. The floor is dirty, and the counter has
mold growing on its edges. Sammy sits down, takes out a
cigarette, and lights up.

"What you need?" he asks. "And who the fuck's that?"
He motions out the door.

"Just a guy," I say. I did call him, but you have to leave
messages for Sammy at the town bar. He doesn't have a
phone, and sometimes he doesn't go in for a week or more.

"You know him?"

"I know him."

"Fine," he says. "What you need?"

"Whatever."

There's a sound outside, a car door slamming, and the
sound of people walking. I hear Trent say hello. Then I hear
someone opening the screen door. It taps against the hinges.
A man is standing there.

"We'd like to rent a canoe," he says.

Sammy looks at me, and I at him, as if we don't understand
the idea of canoes. Two young girls, about seven or so, peer
in the screen door, their hands cupped around their eyes
make their faces look like black splotches.

"Ain't got any," Sammy says.

"There is a sign up on the road," the man says. "It looks
like it needs a little paint, but it says you have canoes and
rafts. Now do you, or is that false advertising?"

He laughs as he says it, and I remember the sign. I
remember painting it with Danny. We spent all day at it,
drank a twelve-pack of Old Milwaukee, and let the sun go
down with the paint still wet. It rained, and Ray made us
paint it again. So we drank another twelve-pack and watched
flies land on the freshly painted sign and stick.

"Don't have any now," Sammy says.

"Well, we drove all the way out here. Can we swim?"

"What the hell," Sammy says. "Hell if I care."

As he goes, I say, "Watch for snakes," and he turns around. "There's snakes," I say. "Just keep your eyes open."

He is outside when I hear one of the girls ask him about snakes, and he tells the girls not to worry about it, that I didn't know what I was talking about. I feel like telling him how I used to work here, right here on this land, and those rotting cabins he'll see down by the water, I built those with my hands. Sammy's looking at me.

"Well?" Sammy says.

"Give me whatever you got," I say, and he goes to a room behind the counter and brings out a few small plastic bags.

"Just cooked it two days ago," he says. "Damn fine shit." He lays the bags up on the table. There are three of them, filled with little crumbles of pills. "I need someone to run up to Illinois to get some anhydrous. I'm low."

"I don't do that," I say.

"It's right there," he says. "I've got maps and everything. Two hundred a quart."

"Two hundred?"

"Two hundred," he says, leaning in, smiling.

"You know," I say, "Ray kept it simple. Pot. That was it. This is getting complicated."

"Too easy to get," Sammy says. "Can you get the ammonia?"

I look back out at the car where I see Trent and think about how he'll jump at the chance. "Yeah," I say, "I think I can swing something."

I give him his take on the last run and put the bags down the front of my pants where I've sewn a pouch just for that purpose. I give Sammy an extra hundred, take a bag of beef jerky, one of the non-perishables for sale on the counter, and go back outside where the sun is nearly gone. I can't imagine how the family would have made a float before dusk. I look at my watch. It's seven thirty. If we leave now, we'll make it back to the city around ten, plenty of time to make a few sales before breakfast. Trent is not in the car, so I go around the general store thinking he may be taking a piss, but I don't see him. I see the cabins down near the river. Water laps the bank near them, and I see where I slept. It's overgrown with weeds and is falling apart. The roof has caved in. I never have looked at it when I've come back. I always go into the store, do my business, and leave without ever looking down at the river the way I used to.

I call out for Trent, but he doesn't respond. Down toward the riverbank, there's splashing, and I can see them in the dusk. There are five of them. The father, the mother, the two girls, and Trent splashing and playing. They are all clothed. In the low light, they look like spirits dancing in the water. I go on down, slowly, taking my time and remembering, with each step, the way the place used to look and how hard it was to keep it that way. I think about the nice ache I used to have in my shoulders and back after a day's work here, and how long it's been since I've felt that kind of solace. The grass is smooth. I can smell the river, the smell of live fish, and I reach the riverbank. Trent sees me.

"Hey," he yells, "the water's great. Look at us."

He doesn't know them. They don't know him, but there he is, mingling, meddling.

"It usually is this time of year."

I pick up a flat stone and toss it sidearm. It catches the surface and skips, flying up river into the setting sun. It dies out just before it reaches a patch of lily pads. The frogs jump off, and the girls squeal.

"That was cool!" they say, and their father is smiling at me.

"That's a pretty good skip," he says.

"Thanks," I say.

"Why don't you come in and swim with us. It's pretty nice," the mother says. She's a small, thin woman, the kind in magazine ads. Her skin is unnaturally brown, except around her shoulders. She has a thin, long neck.

"No," I say. "That's okay." There's simply too much in the water.

"You're missing out," the father says, and he dives under, his body distorted. I can't see his long torso.

I take off my pants, down to my boxers. Off comes my shirt, and I'm in the water standing next to Trent who is splashing himself in the armpits.

"This is all worth it," he says. "This makes everything seem to go away."

I dunk my head under and pull it out. The water flows through my hair, down my neck in little lines that tickle. It does make things disappear. The father pops his head out of the water and yells *SNAKE!* The girls scream and run for shore. Trent and I scream and run, too, and the mother laughs. She has her hands around her shoulders like she's cold, and she's laughing at all of us running around on the bank, slipping on the stones we've made wet with water dripping off our bodies. The girls run in circles. The father comes up out of the water, moving his hands in stiff motions.

"I'm the great river beast," he groans, and the girls scream again. I look up toward the general store where there's a light on now, and I see Sammy sitting on the front porch, smoking and watching us. The father lets out a roar and then stops. He stops and is staring straight down. The girls stop in the silence. They stand with their arms at their sides. He tells them to go to the car. When they protest, he shouts at them, barks like a commander to go to the car. Get in the car, he tells them, and tells his wife to go, too. I go over, and he's standing by my clothes. All the little bags of white powder and pills have spilled out of the pouch and are gleaming in the dusk light. My jeans are right there next to Trent's, the little pocketknife next to the plastic bags. I reach down to pick them up.

"What are you doing?" he asks. His girls aren't in the car. They've stopped just up the hill from the river and are standing with their mother in a little, defensive huddle.

"I'm not doing anything."

"Just what do you think you're doing?"

I study him in the faint light. He's small, thin, and wiry, not a river beast at all.

"It's no big deal," I say.

He steps toward me.

"We don't want any trouble," he says, his voice low so his family can't hear him over the buzz of flies and the river's hum.

"There's no trouble. It's no big deal."

He is close now. Close enough where I can see the curly hair on his chest. I take a step in.

"Calm down now," he says.

I give him a smile. Then I charge him and lift him over my shoulder because I'm bigger. I carry him out into the river. He's thrashing against me, kicking at my stomach, and shouting. I hear his wife and kids screaming. Trent shouts at me to get back here, stop, get back. I dunk the father in the water and hold him under for only a second or so and let him go. He comes up gasping, and I turn to the shore.

"I caught the river beast," I shout. "I caught him."

The girls huddle closer to their mother. They all cry.

"What's wrong?" I say. "I caught the ferocious beast!" I still have a hand on the father's shoulder. When I turn, I splash him in the face. I step away, still splashing, and he runs out of the water the way people do, chugging through it like mud, swaying his thin hips. He gathers his family around him and holds them close. They are all crying. They leave in a tight bunch, moving as one. There's a light on up at the store, and the car stops there. I can see Sammy out on the porch.

"Are you nuts?" Trent asks.

"What's the big deal?" I say.

He reaches down and picks up one of the bags.

"This," he says. "This is the fucking big deal."

I laugh at him. I laugh and laugh and splash the water around me. When I stop, Sammy is standing on the bank with a shotgun in his hands.

"You son of a bitch," he says. "They're calling the cops. One had a goddamn cell phone."

I lay back in the river, let my hair float with the current. I think about the times Danny and I went fishing late at night, the way the moonlight faded into the river. I hear nothing but the sound of water, the light clunks of rocks, and the deep sound of sleep beneath the surface. I'm far away from the bank. What's happening there is no concern of mine.

Man, Woman, Gun

He told me his dog was worth $5000. We were on the front porch that faced an open lot across the street. The dirt blew off the yard and spun in the wind. His wife kept coming out on the porch and offering us water, which we both refused, me because he did. She kept saying, *Don't listen to anything he says. He's an idiot* and going back in the house with the screen door banging behind her. He shook his head each time and shrugged at me.

"Five thousand," he whispered, after she left for a third time, "just to keep a dog."

I was there to buy a gun, a Remington 870 12 gauge with a hex pattern carved into the forestock. I'd called Larry when I found the ad on a local newspaper's Web site. "That's a good gun," Larry had said. The old man hadn't shown me the gun yet, but it was one of those situations where it felt right to let the moment ride, kind of like sitting in front of a sunset with a woman when all you really want to do is kiss the back of her neck and feel her breasts; but there's a way about these things, a way things have to be done. His chair kept creaking, and I could hear the dog underneath the porch scratching around. Little puffs of dust came up through the cracks in the porch's boards.

"He was a hunting dog," the old man said. "Good one. I shot him with that twelve-gauge. I was going to shoot him dead then, but I couldn't. Brought him home instead, and good God almighty what a scene that was."

I mumbled something in agreement.

He said, "I don't think anyone knows much of anything until they've brought home a shot up dog to a wife."

There were rabbits in the open lot, lounging around, munching down the dandelions. They pulled the weeds over and put them in their little mouths. We could see their jaws working as the plant disappeared, slick as rain off tin, down their throats. The old man stood up and stretched. The dog came out from under the porch and up the steps, lifting one leg and pulling up the other.

"That's where he was hit," the old man said. "Right there on the back haunch. Blew his balls off, too." He put his hands on his hips. "Can't even breed anymore," he said, rubbing his head. "Know how valuable it is to have a good old hunting dog to breed?"

I didn't. I'd never owned a hunting dog or a gun. I had seen a few hunting shows on television and thought they were having the kind of time Larry and I would enjoy, something to get us out of the house, away from our wives for a few days in the fall and early winter, the cold right down on our necks, the two of us all connected to the outdoors. But I didn't know anything about it right then, so I said so.

"Damn good thing," he said, looking down at his dog, not touching him. "Damn shame."

He turned and went in the house, and I followed him, the screen door banging behind us, the dog whining, high and tight in the wind.

The gun had a musty shine to it, dull and covered in dust. When he wiped it down with a soft rag, it shone and glistened like new steel. It had an elongated barrel to tighten the spread, he said, and a stock with carved notches.

"Rabbits," he said, pointing at the notches.

He brought the gun out into the living room where his wife sat with crocheting needles resting on her knees. A soap opera blared on the television. He went over and turned it down.

"Damn it," she said under her breath, then began working, her face as dull as the needle's click.

We went to the couch, one on each end.

"I'll sell you this here gun for three hundred dollars," he said.

"The ad said one fifty," I said, reaching in my pocket for the folded and ragged newspaper clipping. I found it two days before and had driven three hours to this little shack of a place in a bump of a town.

"You don't know much, do you?" he said, smiling. "Ads are just a way to get people in. Sucker 'em right through the door and then lynch them for everything they've got. I'll sell it to you for four fifty." He grinned, his teeth dark brown, his eyes milky.

I held up the ad. "Two fifty," I said.

"Shit," he said. He put the gun down on the floor.

"You're a messin' up my floor now," his wife said.

"Jesus, Anna, it don't hurt."

"I'll describe when it hurts," she said and clicked the needles.

Three hours away, my own wife stood at the kitchen window and thought about me. She told me this when I returned, just before I moved out. She said she thought I was in trouble, that I had walked into something I couldn't get out of. It rained while she thought this, and she was so entranced by the feeling, she forgot to close the windows in the front room. It rained in on the carpet. The water stains remained. They are the last thing I remember looking at before I picked up my suitcase and duffel bag and hauled them out to the car.

"Lookee here," the old man said, picking up the gun again. "You can see where it's been crafted by hand." He held it up into the light. He showed me the etch marks where someone had filed the stock so it fit. It didn't look precise.

"Did that myself," he said. "Craftsmanship." He grinned again. He had a way of grinning.

"I won't pay over three hundred," I said. "I can almost buy a new shotgun for that."

"You'll get a piece of shit that won't fire in two years," he said. He pulled out his wallet. "Here," he said, "I'll throw this in for an extra fifty." He pulled out an NRA membership card and held it out to me. I took it and looked it over. "Go on," he said, "take a look. It's real."

"I know it's real," I said.

"Fine organization," he said. He lifted the gun and pointed it, sighted down the barrel. I watched him. He aimed the gun at his wife. She didn't notice. He acted as if he were doing something as normal as brushing his teeth. She didn't turn but stared into her own lap. I thought she might be asleep. He lowered the gun and turned back to me. The needles started again. "Sights as good as the day I bought her."

"You don't sight in a shotgun," I said. I knew that, had read it.

"Sure you do," he said. "What? Think I don't know something about guns? Who you think you are?" He laid the gun across his lap so the barrel pointed at my thigh.

"Point it away," I said, reaching for the barrel.

"It ain't loaded," he said, lifting it so the barrel pointed back over his shoulder. "Here," he held his hand out, "you don't need that card anyhow. Don't need this gun neither. Go on home."

"I came out here to buy the gun," I said. "I'll give you three hundred for it."

"Three fifty," he said.

"Done."

"Three seventy-five," he said, "with the card." He held it up again.

"It's not my membership," I said.

"It's not the membership. It's the card."

"Fine," I said, defeated, "three seventy-five."

I took out my money. It was all I had. I thought of my wife back home and the little nook she had reserved in our living room for one of those freestanding fireplaces. She talked about curling up in front of it, with the dog at our feet, sipping bourbon and coffee. It sounded warm and nice. I took the gun, and the metal felt heavy in my hands.

We had a fight. It lasted much longer than I expected. I stood in the kitchen, at the sink, with warm water and soapsuds all over my hands, looking out the dark window at nothing. Sarah was behind me, breathing so I could hear her. Long pauses shot out from us, tentacles looking for something to cling to. I am one of these people who draws fake lines in the sand. I won't pass here. Here's my limit. I won't go any further than this, and I always do. Always found myself twice as far beyond the line as I could have imagined. Like when we got married, the way the wedding went, and all of that. It was way beyond anything I could have fathomed. This is another one of those times. It's a clear deception, a dance right now, but later it'll be worse. She's backing off. I think I can get a blow in, duck under her uppercut and land one on her soft cheek, but she has this way of breathing that I can't even take. It's like big huffs from an engine, one that is old, chugging on its final limbs. Here I am trying to fix it.

"I'm sorry," I said, a little tired. "It's not a big deal."

"It is a deal if it means anything to you," she said back. I didn't turn around. I grabbed a plate and put it in the water. It disappeared under the soap. The suds jumped up and landed all over the place.

Sometimes I sit up late at night and drink until I think I can remember what was so horrible that night, what drove me to go and say I wanted a gun. I had never said such a thing before, and it wasn't a fight about a gun. I tell myself all the time that it had nothing to do with the gun.

The rest stop was only a few miles from where I got on the Interstate to head home. My cell phone was working now— three new messages. I pulled off onto the shoulder, the gravel running up the wheels and clicking against the chassis. Next to me, the gun shone so clear that my face looked back at me from the barrel's glint. The sky was low over the dead cornfields, lines of clouds rippled like waves. The gun felt heavy and just right in my palm. In my pocket, I could feel the edges of the NRA card digging into my thigh. I got out and felt the air, cool with an inching chill, the kind that moves up your back while your front is warmed by a nice fire. Out over the field, I could see swallows swooping back and forth. I went around, took the gun out, and walked down the embankment into the field. Heavy, black dirt wrapped up around my shoes and white socks. There were four rounds in my pocket, slugs, all included in the three seventy-five.

I took the slugs out and looked them over. There was a little rust on the fire caps, but I thought them good enough. So I loaded them in, one after the other, and I raised up the gun. When I sighted in one of the sparrows, I realized how incredibly powerful I had become. There in the field lay a beer can, crumpled and forgotten. I set it up, walked back twenty paces, raised, aimed, and squeezed.

The can stood like a little flag of rebellion. I watched it stand there, all high and mighty. The dirt exploded around it as I fired again. I looked up. The can still stood. The swallows were gone. The land lay flat and studded with cornstalks. I walked over to the can, my steps purposeful, my gaze focused. When it was at my feet, I stopped and looked down. Its mouth was wide open: big and scared; its thoughts on what might happen. Water collected around its mouth, ran down its sides; I could hear it plead. I had two shells left, and I lowered my barrel down, inches from the can's mouth.

"Open wide," I said, pushing the barrel closer. I held my breath and heard the wind, how it sounded so alone, wanting to rip through cornstalks taller than my head. Instead it was simply blowing by, passing through. I pulled the trigger and did the deed. There was nothing left. I couldn't make out the brand anymore, couldn't tell if it was a Bud or a Miller, and I didn't care. No one would know.

Back in the car, I called my wife and told her I bought a gun. I told her everything.

"I see," she said. "Well, does it work?"

"Of course it works," I said.

"You never can tell," she said. "When you buy things from people, they can screw you over."

"Yes," I said. "But it works. I shot a can."

"How old are you?"

"Old enough," I said, and I hung up. The road lines ran until they were hypnotic and sad in their repetition. I turned on the radio, listened to a Lynyrd Skynyrd song, some Bruce Springsteen, whatever came on. There were headlights in front of me, so many headlights and taillights all stretched out and thin along the Interstate.

Near St. Louis, clouds glowed above the city. Tall buildings huddled in close downtown. Out from there, nothing over four stories except the church steeples, rifling up, all rotten and decrepit. I drove on through it, weaving my way downtown. There are people I know who avoid cities, who drive around them in wide arcs as if avoiding an infection. But I aim myself at the center. As I did all of this, I reached over and rubbed the barrel of the twelve-gauge resting comfortably on the seat beside me.

I turned off the Interstate and onto Broadway, one of the few wide streets blocked in by buildings. It was late, and the traffic was light, a dead downtown. I drove through thinking about the time I wanted to be a police officer and drive up on other people's problems, solve them with a swift move, and drive away. That all changed, though, as most things do.

At a stoplight, I slowed and watched a few homeless people lounge in a doorway. One man got up and came over to the car, looked in the window. He tapped on the glass, and I rolled it down. Spit rain had started to fall. It came in and made my pants damp.

"Got a light?" he asked. He had half a cigarette in his hand, a stump between his fingers. He saw the gun and dropped his smile. He stepped back.

"Yeah," I said. I found the car's lighter, pushed it in. "Got a minute to wait?" He stood by the car, short with sandy hair. I thought about how we must look. The lighter popped out. I held it out to him. "You should be careful on a night like this," I said. "Things can happen."

"You, too," he said, leaning down toward the lighter. "Lots of things go down."

The door was open before I could do anything. He had a friend, this homeless guy, a friend who found my unlocked door, who now had my shotgun, who was standing at the passenger window, the barrel pointed at me. The image of that can in a lonely, sparse cornfield came back, its mouth as wide open as the sky it faced. My jaw danced. I felt warmth between my legs, on the seat.

"Shit," one said, "he's pissed the seat."

"Don't matter," the other said. "Get out," he said to me.

There was one shell in the gun—one slow-moving slug shell that could blow a hole in my back, taking everything important with it. I got out of the car, my legs aching.

"Go on," said the one with the gun. I kept looking up and down the street for someone. A huge city with lights and buildings all lit up all night and nothing. Not a cop. Not a car. Nothing. Just paper bags dancing by like ignorant observers. I sat on the curb. The men were in my car with the gun between the seats where I could see the barrel up near the one's ear, the guy who had found my passenger door unlocked. They drove away and looked normal going down the street. Normal as a can. Normal as a $5000 dog with no balls.

I called the police. I called my wife.

"I was carjacked," I said.

"Jesus," she said. "Jesus."

"I'm all right," I said, shaky now. "Except for my pants. I wet myself."

"Jesus," she said. "Where are you?"

"St. Louis," I said. "Almost home."

"I'll come get you," she said.

"They took everything," I said. "They took the gun."

She didn't answer. We were disconnected. Or maybe she hung up. I looked at all the things around me, trying to assess what I should have done. The paper blowing by, the steam rising ghostlike from the manhole covers, as steady as my wife's breath. The glass doors of the building across the street, deep and dark, locked and quiet. My hands were cold from where I had them on the sidewalk. I took the NRA card out of my pocket and studied it. The old man's name was signed in wobbly hand across the bottom. *Ferald James Haney*. I put it back in my pocket, the plastic hard on my legs. It would take Sarah at least an hour to reach me. I had it all figured out. But here I was, wounded, cold, alone. A cop car turned onto the street, its lights blazing like fire. It pulled up next to me. The cop got out, came over, picked me up by my arms, and started asking me questions. He asked me if I'd been drinking. If I had any drugs on me. I said no. No drugs. No drinking. They'd stolen my car. My gun.

"You had a gun?" he said. "Why didn't you use it?"

I didn't answer him. I could only think of the wide open mouth of a can, sitting in pieces among hacked cornstalks, of me and Larry, with guns over our shoulders tromping through a forest, drinking beer, laughing at sex jokes. And then my wife, in our Chevy Suburban with the gray interior, driving down long lines of Interstate doodled on a map like ink drippings, her eyes red from the halos she always sees at night.

Everything Has Its Place

At night, when Connie comes home, we sit together on the terrace and talk about our day. I tell her about my time in the mailroom, sorting the mail for the *Chicago Sun-Times*. She tells me about her book signing, her meeting with her agent, or something else more extravagant than anything I have to say. The terrace is cool in the evenings, and we like to have a drink or two and watch the sun go down. It's nice to see it low over Chicago. Its rays fall on the lake, cut through the buildings in wide slants, and make things solemn. The traffic noise and the smog disappear in those moments. Then it is just us with the falling sun.

After stuffed crab cakes, something we ordered in, Connie suggests we clean up the mess and go for a dip in the rooftop pool. She takes what is left on her plate and dumps it over the railing where it falls thirty-two stories before landing on the sidewalk.

"You shouldn't do that," I say. "It could hit someone."

"It's good for them," she says. "I'm helping people."

My wife has a fake regard for the importance of life. For a sex novelist, she has very little idea of what sex means, at least in my view. She writes books with titles like *Hearts*

Afire and *Steamy City*. Some have been bestsellers, and she has a fan base of women I will never meet. I assume they all live underground in some vast cave. I imagine them crowded in little rooms, all alone, with black light bulbs to read by. They eat only when Connie feeds them. Connie says I have no idea what goes on with a writer, that I don't have any clue at all what it takes, and I've never even read one of her books. That's true. I haven't. I would be afraid I'd show up somewhere, I suppose. The man with the small penis? But it's more than that. That my wife has ideas scares me, mostly because I know her too well.

We're back inside. Connie takes off her clothes and stands naked by the window, looking out on the city where the lights are popping up like champagne bubbles.

"It's funny," she says, "how the city looks like it grew right from the ground."

"Someone built it," I say.

"But it doesn't look that way."

"A city planner designed it that way. Are you going swimming?"

She pulls on her bathing suit and sits down in a chair, stretches out her long legs, and crosses her ankles. She is stunning, but there's not much left of her after that. She's always tan and lean.

"I want to smoke," she says.

"You can when we get back."

Connie takes a towel off the heated rack, and we go out the door, up the stairs to the elevator that we take to the top floor. The outside air is cooler, but not cold enough to warrant swimming inside, so we find two chairs.

Christmas lights dangle from their strands. Lights underneath the water make the ripples flash as they roll in and out of shadows made by swimmers. A little beetle scampers past my toes on its way to a potted plant. It climbs over the cracked concrete, pulling itself toward home.

Connie and I sit together, and I watch as people approach, one at a time, and talk with her as if she is a long-time friend.

"How's the new book?" one woman asks. She's wearing an angular red bathing suit that hugs her hips and makes her all curvy.

"It's just grand," Connie says, her index and middle finger held in a way that suggests she is smoking.

"I can't wait to read it. What's this one about? Jarod? Does Jarod show up? God, I love Jarod."

"Yes, Jarod is in there."

A man snakes up behind the woman in the red swimsuit. "Who's Jarod?" he asks.

The woman spins around. "Tommy," she squeals. "So good to see you. Jarod is the character I'm absolutely in love with. This is Connie Weathers. She writes. She's a writer."

"Nice to meet you, Connie Weathers," the man says.

The woman says, "Connie keeps me excited about reading. She really has a knack for words." Then she says, "We all read her books," and motions over her shoulder to a group of people standing near the building's edge. The small cluster remains close, guarding each other from people they don't know or don't care to talk to.

It isn't long before I feel like diving in where all the conversation becomes gagged and muffled.

I have never lived like this. Before Connie started selling her books, we lived in Collinsville, Illinois—a little hole of a town across the river from St. Louis. We made no money or very little. I worked as a part-time dealer on a gambling boat, and Connie worked at a nearby ketchup factory. Where she got her stories, I don't know.

We were simple. Bare bones. I always thought we'd move along just like that through life, etching out a living, raising a family, making our way through the world as fast as Collinsville would allow. But an agent called, Connie signed a contract, and we ended up moving to the city. Later, when it became obvious to my wife that St. Louis couldn't hold her, we packed up and headed off to Chicago and this lush apartment.

I went out for a job mostly because I couldn't stand looking out over the city every day through a haze. The job was much like dealing blackjack. Each card had a value. If I kept track of the values, I could discern the odds. Everything fit into little places like cubbyholes on a desk.

Sometimes I think about all of this when I'm floating on my back, looking up into a blank sky. I can see airplanes approaching Midway and O'Hare, and I think they are all a little like me, way up with nothing to see.

I look over and see Connie talking to Donald Dobson, the big real estate man who always speaks in code. He is leaning over her. I swim to the edge and shake his hand. His shake is weak as if he doesn't consider me on any level.

"I'm looking into some new property," he says. "You two should get in on the ground floor. I'm always up for taking on partners."

"We'll do that," Connie says.

There are more people now. They've come up for family night. Torches are lit around the pool. The torch light shimmers on the water. Children run and ignore the signs. The staff sets up two bars and begins serving complimentary drinks.

"Get me a vodka tonic," Connie says to me. "What'll you have, Don?"

Don doesn't say anything but smiles at her. He gives me a strange look, one that shows me what he's thinking, that he'd like to have my wife alone for a moment if I didn't mind. It's something not done much here where your clothes, your hair, the way you order your drink meld together to create a skin you walk around in and wear like a heavy coat. To let your guard down, to shed that skin and become exactly who you are, is not tolerated. People have been evicted for it.

The poolside grows louder. I go to the bar and ask for a vodka tonic. The bartender pours it and hands it to me. I instinctively go for my wallet, even in my trunks, but I stop myself before it is obvious that I don't know what I'm doing. Even after living here four months, I feel as if things around me are happening without my being a part of them. It's as if I'm in the front row at a movie theater. I watch the kids run around the pool. The adults, loud and laughing, spit over the building's side. The bartender pours another drink and hands it to me, but I can't feel it. It's not cold or hot. It's just there like a fog you can't feel even when it's all around you.

Later when we're back on our own terrace, I say to Connie, "What's the deal with that Don Dobson?"

She cocks her head and smiles her half-faced smile—the one where her right eyebrow moves up into a broad arch and her right eye glistens and gets large. Meanwhile, the left side of her face stays numb and expressionless, even falls a little into a frown.

"You're jealous of his money. That's all," she says and takes a long draw on her cigarette, blows smoke out into the night.

"I'm not."

"You are," she says. She touches my leg as if to reassure me she knows what she's talking about.

Below us, thirty-two stories down, Chicago is alive and well and moving. We can hear the faint sounds of taxi horns, but mostly we hear the wind blowing off Lake Michigan and swirling up around us. Lake Shore Drive is lit up now like a thin yellow snake twisting its way along the shoreline. I can see the new pavilion, Grant Park, and beyond it the soft lights around Shedd Aquarium and Soldier Field looking as if they are anchored in a bay. I know all these things, yet I know little else about the city, having not gone much further than the *Chicago Sun-Times*. This makes me feel as useless as driftwood. Connie touches my leg again; this time she shakes it.

"You were thinking?"

"No," I say.

"You were. What about?"

"I was thinking about the way we used to go to the corner bakery in Collinsville and buy a gallon of homemade ice cream and take it home and eat the whole thing."

"Well," she says, "we always had plenty of ice cream."

"Yeah."

"And ketchup," she says. We are laughing again in an old way. She tosses her cigarette over the side. Together we watch it fall, tumbling over itself in the wind, spinning and burning, always diminishing, a dying star on a thirty-two-story fall.

After we make lazy love on the bed, we sit up for a while and watch late night QVC and remark on the obscure products being sold. We watch a sports collectible show and see a small statue of Mickey Mantle being offered for $600. I think about how everyone in the building could afford that statue and how frivolous that seems. The television's glow blocks out the windows, makes it hard to see out, locks us in its steady stream. I reach over for Connie. When I discover she is asleep, I go to the kitchen and make myself a sandwich.

I haven't adjusted to our new eating habits: light breakfast, no lunch, light dinner. I use lettuce, mayonnaise, bologna, ham, mustard, and pickles piled high—Dagwood-style— and carry it into the living room where I eat it while standing near the window. The city stretches for miles. I can see the lights in the distance and realize I've never been there, though I can see *there*, and I never will go.

It is then that I see a fireball coming down out of the sky in a gentle descent. It is small, but it grows larger until I can see it clearly. It is an airplane, swooping in over the city and on fire. I have an instinct to wake Connie, but I don't. I stay at the window most of the night, watching out toward O'Hare airport.

The crash is all over the news. Connie and I can't stop watching the TV coverage. Apparently, there was a malfunction of some sort, but no one can confirm anything. The conspiracy theorists say it was a botched attack, but the experts disagree.

"From this vantage point," the expert says, "it looks like an unfortunate accident. I have nothing to say otherwise."

From *this* vantage point, I think; it was as though some Zeus-like god reached down and touched us.

Behind the on-camera reporter is a massive pillar of smoke, which we can also see from our window, rising up from O'Hare. It's a strange combination of the real and the imagined. Connie, beside me, shakes. She keeps looking at the television, out the window, and back again.

"It's so unreal," she says and gets up to make breakfast.

They show the plane coming down again from the airport sky camera. It is usually used to show us the weather and the hazy outside world, but now it has transformed into an information device, delivering us all the images we've never wanted to see. The plane comes down much too fast and explodes on impact, creating a ball of fire that shoots up and momentarily blinds the camera. When things clear, there is nothing on the ground but smoke, fire, and twisted metal. Later, fire trucks arrive and begin spraying water on the blaze. Police cars quarter off the airport, and the news anchor tells us someone from the FBI is flying in from Washington to assist the local office.

I go over and look out our window and see the streets below jammed with cars. The city seems not to have noticed. It moves along in the way it always should, without stopping to consider the magnitude of what happens to it. I think the planner had that in mind when the streets were laid out, the way they allow for diversion and how you can get lost in them without thinking, without seeing anything but what's right in front of you. There are places where I wouldn't be able to see the smoke. If I were down on the ground floor, everything would be blocked. Up here, above the fray, I can see everything.

We get a note in the mail two days later saying the Community Board has convened a mandatory meeting to decide what to do in case of an emergency. I crinkle my brow at Connie.

"An emergency?"

"They want to be prepared," she says.

We go to the fifth floor where there are no condos, only four smaller meeting rooms, one large ballroom, and a small swimming pool. This area is for parties. The room is full, and there are people I've never seen before. Connie peels away from me, headed for a group. I spot Don Dobson and go over to him.

"Quite a turnout," I say.

"What do you expect?"

Someone comes over and whispers in his ear, and he nods.

"Did you see it?" I ask.

"No."

"I did. I saw it."

"You should get a medal," he says. "Where's your wife?"

I motion over my shoulder.

"That woman has a real knack for words," he says.

I didn't know he'd read any of her books. I ask him about it.

"I've read a few. Hot stuff. Must be fun being you."

I laugh with him but put little behind it.

The meeting starts with an older man rapping a gavel on a podium. He calls everyone to order and reminds them to get something to drink and eat. It's all free, of course, but he doesn't say this. It's expected. Then he begins by saying how sorry he is for all the victims, how it will be years before we will be able to put this tragedy behind us and move on, and how he expects each of us to do our part and donate to already established charities. He has already donated $10,000.

"Remember to donate," Connie whispers into my ear.

Then the old man begins reading a few notes from previous meetings. The Community Board meets once per month, and all the residents receive the meeting minutes in their mailboxes. They usually decide things such as the decibel level at which doorbells can ring or what color welcome mats are acceptable. Sometimes they quell disputes between two resident pets. They settled the matter of Starky vs. Mittens, a case of a dog and cat disliking each other, which sparked some debate. This is far above their usual capacity.

In the ballroom, a long row of high windows looks out across Michigan Avenue where our view is abruptly blocked by another building. It's nice.

"Now," the old man says, "we come to the matter at hand. We need to know what we would do in case of a disaster here at Gardens in the Sky Tower."

"It could've been us," a woman says from the crowd. "They could've been aiming at us."

It's obvious she's drunk, and people shush her.

"Yes," the old man says and raps his gavel. "Yes, that's what we're here to discuss."

Through the windows I can see out into the city where the sun is fading in. Window washers, wearing white suits that make the men stand out, scale the building across the street like tiny bugs flattened against the wall. They work the squeegees in angular motions while the drunken lady shouts, "We can't be too careful," and I think about how hot it will get outside. Connie and I are near the back of the room, so I stand up and move over to the window where I can look around the corner and down Michigan Avenue. It opens up not far from the building's corner, right after it crosses Randolph. Don is near the window, looking at the same things I am and twirling a highball glass so the ice clinks.

"I only live in high rises," he says. "The only way to get away from anything is to live above it. You know, look down on it like you're a god."

I know what he means, but I don't like it at all. I don't like the looks of the little men washing windows. There is something distorted about seeing things from this height, as if everything is pristine and clean like new shoes or that everything exists as it does in our conference room with perfect fake plants and sterile, condensed, and filtered air.

The old man at the podium shouts about safety regulations. He has a map and points out where the proper stairwells are in case of a fire.

"You should go here," he says, aiming a laser pointer. The little red dot falls on the map and shakes. It's difficult to tell exactly where we are supposed to go.

"We'll all go to hell," the drunken lady says, though not as loud now. People have managed to control her.

Don says to me, "You really should look into that property. It would be good for you to get in on the ground floor."

Connie comes over. "You shouldn't be lounging near the window," she says. "This is important."

I go over and sit with her, and she crosses her legs and puts her hand in mine. It's cold in the room, much colder than I had originally thought.

The next morning, I'm up before the sun. Connie placed the minutes from the meeting on my bedside table. Those minutes had drawled on and eventually put me to sleep last night.

I go over to the window where I can see down into the street if I press my forehead against the cold glass. My head makes a ring of condensation. I can see a few cars, their headlights thrown out like spears, and I can see the morning sun reflecting through the glass of the next building over. We're above its roof, and there are people up there this morning doing aerobics, practicing Tai Chi, and running around a track. They have plants up there, too. A whole garden was lifted right out of the dirt and planted in concrete. The people keep running as the sun comes up.

I hear Connie behind me. She's moaning a little, her sleep slipping off. At these little moments, before she's awake, before the sun comes up, I like to think of her as she once was: a small girl in a small town. I try to remember what our dreams were, what we talked about during hot nights in our little apartment in Collinsville.

We have moved from the bedroom to the living room where we are on the couch together. She runs her hands through her hair and rubs her eyes. We move slowly like the jets coming in. They inch from where we see them, but way up they are hurtling through the air, nothing to stop them except hope and brakes. We have neither.

"Don wants you to look at those apartments with him today," Connie says. "Will you go?"

"What about work?"

"What about it? You can miss it. Call them."

"It's not that easy," I say.

"It's a silly job. You should quit."

"I can't," I tell her.

"Sure you can. It's easy. 'Hello, I quit.' You make things too hard for people."

I tell her that I'll go with Don because it makes life easier to tell her what she wants to hear.

I'm waiting for Don in the hotel bar.

"I'm leaving my wife," I tell a man next to me. He is wearing a tweed suit, and he is a little older. There is an angled look about him, chiseled, as if he has seen enough.

"Done that," he says. "The other way around though."

He is drinking rum and Coke. He orders another, tells the bartender to hold off on the Coke this time. When the drink comes, he takes it all at once.

"I'm kidding," I say.

"Just don't kill anyone," he says and gets up to leave. At the door, a few men slap him on the back.

Don comes in. He is wearing a gray suit and a silk tie. He smells like aftershave, hair gel, and soap. All his smells mix together in a nice way with the bar smoke and beer. It makes me think he planned it, right down to his smell.

"It's a good day to look at these," he says, handing me a brochure.

The apartments are a five-story building in the shape of an "H." I can see where the swimming pool could be. Don points out the roof, how it is perfect for a tennis court.

"Way up there," Don says. "Playing tennis with the gods."

"Doesn't that get old?" I asked.

"Heaven's no," he laughs.

"It looks like a hospital," I say.

"I think it was. You ready?"

I'm ready. We go out into the morning heat. Out on the

lake, the gulls are high over the water, and a few clouds hang like pictures.

We are in the car when Don says, "Look, I'm wondering what it will take to get you out of the building."

"Out of the building?"

"You're a nuisance. You don't belong there."

A line of cars goes past with a hearse at the front.

"Crazy devils," Don says. "They think the dead want to see the water one more time."

I watch the lake sweep past Don's car window. His driver glances back, his eyes on me.

"What's this all about?" I ask.

"You know," Don says, "I always like to think about the stories in a place. Every place has stories. Stories that fit into it just right, like mail into a slot. But you don't fit. Your story doesn't belong."

"Yours does?"

"Most likely," he says. "If all the pieces fit. It's an offer, that's all. Take it or leave it."

"What offer?"

"This," he says, handing me the brochure again.

"The apartments?"

"For God's sake," he says, "an apartment. One apartment for you leaving. Said and done."

"You'll give me an apartment if I leave?"

"Sure. You get the apartment. I get what you have."

"Connie."

"Of course."

He has a small smile on his face. His black hair is creased with greasy gel and looks wet but is crisp and dry. The lake behind him moves in slow motion. The gulls float.

"Here," he says. "Here are these apartments."

Inside, I find myself staring out a large, plate-glass window overlooking the lake. The living room and dining room are one, but the kitchen is set off and has a serving area cut out of the wall. There is a long hallway off to our left leading to, Don says, two bedrooms and a bathroom. The rooms are cut like cookies out of the old hospital layout with few right angles. Corners jut out and make sharp turns back, less than ninety degrees.

"It's like Shangri-la," Don smirks. Mud is all over the carpet, and I notice one side of the window is busted out. Don twirls around in the living room.

"Triggers," Don says. He points at the smoke alarm. "Just a trigger. Like that airplane. Triggered the meeting, triggered me talking to you, triggered us being here, me offering you the place. Triggers."

He stops, lights a cigarette underneath the smoke alarm, holds it up. Nothing. "What do you think? Think you can make this work?"

I hear the slight sound an envelope makes when it slides into a mail slot, the sound a card makes as a player turns it over for a blackjack. I go into the kitchen where I start rummaging through the drawers. There are little piles of mouse droppings, and the drawers are lined with apple-red shelf paper. The floor was once white linoleum. Inside a drawer, I find a pair of old scissors, the metal kind with long, thin blades. I lift them up to my face and can see the rust spots that appear dabbed on, as with a brush. Out the window, I see Don's car parked near the front door. There are things that are so much more than triggers.

Back out in the living room, I open the closets and then go down the hall to the bathroom and find it has been used recently. The toilet is clogged. The bedrooms are spacious. The hallway carpet is surprisingly clean as I walk on it in the cool dark and slip the scissors in my back pocket. Don is in the living room with his little smile curled around his nose like twin hooks. There is plenty of room in the little place.

Scrapping a Bird

If you were to come upon them, you'd find them under the new bridge where the river reflected off the steel girders in ripples. The air blew through like a tunnel, and the boys drew their coats up close and held their beer cans in gloved hands. Not one of them was older than eighteen.

Earlier that day, they had been hunting quail on Dennis Stance's farm south of Wynott. The dogs picked the birds up well. Their breath froze around their faces, and they chased two coveys all day, taking seven birds between the four of them. Now they slumped around the fire, knotted together like a hay bale.

"Good day," one said. The others agreed.

The dead quail were piled up near the fire and dressed; they planned to cook them and eat them later. Someone would have to eat only one because Eddie had busted a bird apart as it flew not five feet from the end of his twelve-gauge. *Not a hunt without Eddie scrapping a bird*, they'd said, but now someone would have to do without, and it would probably be Eddie. Not because he was the one who busted the bird, but because he never looked like a person who had anything to him. He was only a sliver, a slip of the tongue they sometimes let out, and that's how they mentioned him. *Eddie's coming, too*, they'd say.

Eddie's father owned and operated the pool hall in town, and he would go there after school and play for the house. He got good. Real good, and that gave him some standing, but not with the boys at school. His father didn't allow boys younger than nineteen into the pool hall, which meant Eddie spent most of his time around people he couldn't relate to at all, who talked about things he didn't understand. He knew things that the others didn't, such as the horrible war, the protests, the signs around town calling for a new vote for mayor. He knew all the things he really didn't care to know and didn't know anything about the stuff he really wanted to know about. Baseball. Who would buy beer and cigarettes. Girls. He could talk about all the things the men at the pool hall knew with such clarity it made it sound as if he actually knew what he was saying, but he never could say a word about anything that mattered to the boys standing around him.

"We need some wood," Lionel said. Lionel had a slim build, slim arms, bone-thin hands. He looked like he could break in half if the wind blew just right, but Lionel's quickness dumbfounded everyone. He moved in flashes.

"Yeah," a freshman said. There were two of them. Lionel kept them around for booze money, for getting wood, for anything.

"Go get some," he said.

They went, so Lionel and Eddie were alone. Lionel took out a pack of cigarettes and handed them over. Eddie took one and lit it with a piece of dried wood that flamed on one end.

"Good night," Lionel said.

"Yeah," Eddie said.

They sat down on the rocks.

"Shouldn't be long before people start showing up."

"Kind of nice like this," Eddie said. "Quiet and all."

"You're a real kick, Eddie."

Lionel picked up a rock and tossed it in the direction the freshmen had gone. Eddie did the same. They didn't hear a response.

"You figure out what you're going to do?" Eddie asked.

"Yeah," Lionel said. "I'm going to work for my uncle, I guess."

Lionel's uncle owned a clothing store in town, and Lionel worked there in the summer.

"I'll probably take it over someday. Throw that old bastard out on his ass."

"Old fart," Eddie said.

"Old fuck," Lionel corrected.

"Yeah," Eddie said.

The freshmen came back and dropped the wood on the fire, which smoldered and smoked under the cold, damp wood. Then it caught, jumped up at them, and lit up the bridge's underside. They could hear the cars rumbling over the bridge, coming down the turnoff, and crunching the gravel. The headlights threw light all over the place.

Eddie felt a little wheezy, so he stopped drinking. After a while, Lionel came up to him, put his arm around him, and spoke in his ear.

"You got your truck?"

"Yeah," Eddie said.

"Let's get the hell out of here."

"Why?"

"Cause," Lionel said, "this place gives me the creeps."

Voices echoed off concrete and came back in shades no one understood. Eddie found the two freshmen and told them to come on. They piled in the truck, and Lionel came in after them with a girl in tow.

"This is Shelly," he said.

"Hey," they said. They knew her. She was from another town. She was small and had a thin face that sucked in around her cheekbones, making her all angled in the firelight that still came through the pickup's window. Her string-thin hair rose and fell with the wind that blew through the open windows. Eddie started the truck.

"Where we going?" he asked.

"The Hill," Lionel said.

The freshmen rode in the back; their shoulders hunkered low against the cold. The girl sat between him and Lionel. She had her hands between her legs. She laughed when they said things and asked questions about their hunt. They drove five miles and then turned off the highway. Trees lined each side. They bumped along until they came to the spot near where the creek crossed the road. Eddie stopped.

"It'll be high," he said. "We shouldn't try it."

"Fine by me," Lionel said. He turned to the girl. "What about you?"

"Cool," she said.

Eddie watched as the freshmen spilled out the back. They were both drunk. Taking them home would be a problem.

"This is fantastic," Lionel said. "The whole world belongs to us." He let out a scream and ran down to the creek, which was up. He ran out in it, getting his clothes wet.

"That's not a good idea," Eddie said.

"Hell with it," Lionel said. He beckoned to the freshmen and the girl. "Come on in. The water's just fine."

They followed, and Eddie stood on the bank watching the four of them splash around in the icy water. He felt the shivers crawling all over him. They stayed out there until they began to feel the ache.

"We should build a fire," Eddie said.

"Good idea," Lionel said. "You do that."

They stood against the pickup. The girl sat inside with

the heater running, aimed at her legs. Eddie went and gathered the wood, stacked it, and lit it. The flames began rolling. Nothing a fire can't fix, Eddie thought. It's not that cold. They gathered around the fire, and the girl came out and joined them. Eddie looked at them. They were wet up to their waists, and they shifted from one foot to the other as they tried to pound the feeling back in.

"We can take shifts in the truck," Eddie said. "Everyone can spend a little while under the heater and then come back out here to the fire. We'll be warm enough."

"We'll be fine," Lionel said. "My God, Eddie," he said, "what would we do without you?"

"Freeze to death," Eddie said.

"No," Lionel said. "I mean, really. How could we get along without you?"

"I guess you couldn't," Eddie said.

"You're damn right we couldn't." Lionel looked at the freshmen, at the girl. "I mean, we'd all be dead out here if it weren't for you."

"I don't know about that," Eddie said. He pulled his coat up around his neck.

"You're the damn savior," Lionel said.

Eddie didn't say anything. Part of him didn't care. He liked it, the compliments and praise, something he only got from the older men down at the pool hall when he beat them fair and square. Even if it came from Lionel, in that voice. He could tell they were drying out because they sat down and pulled their legs up close. The girl sat close to Eddie, leaning over on him a little.

"That was really stupid," she said. "Why'd we do something like that?" She shivered against him. Lionel got up and walked away, saying he had to piss.

"It's him," Eddie said. "He does things, and people follow him."

"You don't," she said.

"Yes I do. Sometimes I do."

"You seem nice," she said.

"I guess," Eddie said. "That's all what people see."

"So, why do you hang out with him?"

Eddie paused. The bright embers pulsated, and sparks shot from the wood as one of the freshman tossed a rock into the flames.

Eddie said, "Some of the things I've done, I can't believe I've done them, but it's all because of him," he said, gesturing off toward the woods. "I've jumped off cliffs, raced cars, lit firecrackers off under a person's window, been in fights, gotten drunk. Think I'd do anything like that without him?"

"I don't know," she said. "You seem like the kind of person who doesn't need that."

"I do," he said. "I wouldn't be much of anything without it."

"You might," she said.

Things stayed quiet for a while. They lounged around and watched the fire die.

"Some hunt today," Eddie said.

"Yeah," Lionel said. "Why don't you cook those birds?"

Eddie went to the truck where the freshmen had piled the birds near the tailgate. He picked up one and moved its stiff, skinned leg. The meat felt cold, and it was dotted with feathers where they couldn't get them off.

"They need washing," Eddie said.

"So wash 'em," Lionel said.

Eddie thought of giving the birds to the freshmen, sending them down to the creek to do it, but then he took the birds and went to the water. He put his hands down in it and felt the chill rush up his arm fast as lightning through a tree. The first bird took longer because it had the guts still in. He pulled them out, tossed them aside, crouched near the water, and washed the insides all out. He'd have to find something to use as a spit or at least a stick to hold the birds over the fire. They would need more wood. He turned his head and could see the four of them up around the fire, their faces lit up, talking. Eddie washed the second bird, the next, and the next. The whole time his hands were shaking. He beat his hands against his legs for warmth, but that made his pants wet and his thighs cold.

The little creek was way up. It covered the road. Soon it would freeze over and be still. But now it ran through hard. In the moonlight, he could see the branches and twigs as they crossed the road in the current, headed downstream to meet the river where they'd slow and catch on something. Eddie thought how nice that sounded, to jump in and be carried away and just catch on somewhere else, a new place with a new view. He cleaned another bird. Yes, he thought, that would be nice in some ways. Behind him, he heard Lionel laugh. Then the freshmen joined in. They were all so stuck to him.

He went back to the fire, found a couple of sticks, and handed them to the freshmen after he'd whittled down the ends to a point. They stuck the birds and put them over the fire. Soon the meat began to whistle.

"Now," Lionel said, "this is living." He looked over at the girl who sat between him and Eddie. He reached out for her, but she moved away, closer to Eddie. Lionel stood up and took her arm. "Come on," he said. She pulled back and drew her coat up around her neck. Lionel reached down and took her under the arms.

She said, "No," then, but Lionel didn't seem to listen. He had her by the arm in his quick grip and pulled her off toward the creek. She looked back at Eddie, the firelight draining on her face.

"Aren't you going to help me?" she said.

The two freshmen grinned at one another. Eddie thought of branches floating away and quail fluttering in the sky and didn't move. He held his stick and watched until the bird burst into flames and fell off into the fire. They could hear them down by the creek near the water, so close that sometimes they heard a little splash at first as the girl struggled.

Lionel called, "Send them boys down here," and the two freshmen got up together and walked out of the firelight toward the creek.

Eddie waited. He heard the wet wood pop and fizzle as it caught and felt the cold rocks digging into his legs, the dirt gathering around his ankles. He thought he saw something moving in the woods, a glint of something metal, but it was nothing, only his eyes and the moon. He reasoned every one of his senses betrayed him. Then the freshmen came back and sat down. They smiled at one another.

One said, "He's having another go. Then we'll get out."

The other said, "He said for you to come on down if you want."

Eddie didn't say anything to them.

"Relax man," the first one said. "She's a whore. Everyone knows it. She likes this kind of stuff."

Eddie didn't see that at all, but he'd heard the stories about the girl. They had never been here before, though, not this far off the map. They had tried lots of things. But this took Eddie to a different place.

"Nothing's going to happen," one freshman said. "She won't say a damn thing."

"What do you know?" Eddie asked.

The freshman looked at him across the fire. Eddie still had his skewer stick. It was charred on one end. He pointed it at the freshman.

"You little shit," he said. "What do you know?"

"Same as you," the freshman said, and he stood up, picked up a rock. Eddie looked at him, his young face, the rock in his hand. He dropped his stick. The freshman kept the rock and tossed it in the air and caught it. He told the other one how he would start in center for the varsity baseball team next year.

"Killer arm," he said. He gunned the rock. It went by Eddie's head so close he could feel its breeze, and it struck a tree behind him. "Accurate, too." They both laughed and sat on the ground with their arms wrapped around their legs.

"We've just got to wait a few minutes," one said. "He'll be done soon."

"What about her?" the other one asked.

"I don't know," the one said. "Guess she was done a while ago."

"She'll just stay out here?" the other one said.

"Yeah," his friend said. "She's done this before. Didn't you hear about it? With Eckers and Davidson and all them?" The other one said no, he hadn't heard. "Yeah, all of them. Down here, too." He lit a cigarette. The cold made the end glow. "They said she wanted to stay out here. Didn't want to be seen with all of them. You didn't hear? Ask Davidson about it in gym. He'll tell you."

Lionel came back.

"Get in the truck," he said. The two freshmen got up and piled in the back.

"What happened?" Eddie asked.

"Just get in the truck, Ed."

"Where is she?"

Lionel shoved Eddie back against the pickup. He hit the fender and the breath went out of him.

"Start the goddamn truck," Lionel said.

Eddie stood up, holding his chest. He wasn't sure where he was at first. He saw the fire, saw the sticks lying around.

He opened the heavy truck door and got in, started it up, and turned on the headlights. As they flashed across the creek, he thought he saw a red jacket tangled in the branches.

He took the freshmen home first. Then he dropped off Lionel.

Lionel said, before he got out, "Don't say anything. Not a fucking word. We weren't anywhere tonight."

"What happened?" Eddie asked again.

"Not a word," Lionel said. He got out and went into the house. Eddie watched as the lights came on. Through the front bay window, he saw Lionel's mother come in and give him a hug. Lionel hugged her back and sat down on the sofa, flipped on the television.

For a while, Eddie drove around Wynott. He sat for a long time watching the flashing red light burst and fade. The town lay still and silent. There were a few lights on in people's houses and a few houses where people had forgotten to turn off the porch light. All the signs of life, but nothing moved much. Only the flashing red light and a few cars, people coming home from third shift at the tractor parts factory over in Harrison, where the girl lived. He saw a few people he knew and waved to them to show that things were normal. They waved back but didn't stop. It was late, a time of night when you didn't stop to talk to anyone even if you wanted to.

He drove out of town and down to the new bridge where earlier that night they'd stood and had a beer and talked about the hunt. He thought about that. He thought about how young he felt all the time. A few people still lingered around, and he stopped up the road and watched from a distance. The fire had gone down, and the people around it were shadows. They were smoking and talking in low voices, and he could see them touching one another in the dark, moving their hands over each other. He watched them until they began getting up and going into their trucks. The cab lights dwelled on them for a moment, lighting their faces as they came together. Then the lights went out. The fire remained, a dull red dot against the black river, as pointless as a cigarette butt.

He drove over to the creek. As he came around the bend, he saw the girl sitting on a stump near the water, her jacket held up close to her face. The headlights fell on her, and she tried to hide in her jacket. He could see that she wasn't wearing any shoes. Then he could see she only had the jacket.

Eddie got out and went over to her. When he touched her, she winced and pulled away. He reached down and took her up under her arms. She lifted easily; it was like picking up a small stone. He led her to the truck and put her inside.

He blasted the heater, hoping that would warm her up. She didn't say anything. He looked down at her legs, all covered in slick blood made black in the dark.

"It's all right," he kept saying to her, but she wouldn't look at him, wouldn't say anything back. "Tell me what they did," he said. "Tell me everything so I'll know."

They pulled onto the main road. She laid her head over on his lap. He could feel tears making his leg cold, and he fought the tingle between his legs. She kept her head there, and he drove into the night toward Harrison. The full moon lit and shadowed the clouds, stretched in thin lines like hurdles across the sky. Twenty-seven miles. He had plenty of gas to get there. He didn't know about getting back.

Cold Start

As the sun set and made long shadows of cedars stretch across the dirt road, Harold watched Jacob Handerham walk by. Harold sat on his front porch, his rocking chair creaking as he moved. Jacob stopped and dawdled near the ditch, as if he were stalking a toad to catch in a jar and to feed flies to. He picked up a stick and carried it with him as he went down the road.

Harold knew the boy, knew his father better, and didn't think much of either. They were both wet around the ears as farmers. Baling their hay too green. Overfeeding their cattle. Then underfeeding them. The kinds of things that came up around the cast iron stove at the Missouri Farmers Association meeting, after the official business was all heard.

The sun christened the sky with a bright pink drop, the color of Christmas candy he had eaten as a child. He pulled out his father's pipe, packed it, lit it, puffed, and smoked. He licked his teeth. The tobacco's sweet taste matched the sky. Jacob Handerham was gone, and Harold felt tired in his bones. He went inside, ate a supper of black beans and bread, and went to bed.

◆ ◆ ◆

It was the smell that woke him. The windows were open. A light breeze pushed a cold front eastward, smelling first of rain and then of the harsh smell of burning grass. Harold tumbled out of bed and went to the window where he drew the ruby-red curtains his wife had sewn. He saw the lines of hay bales across the road, the ones just on the other side of the fence, aflame.

Before he knew what he was doing, he spun toward the empty bed and shouted, "Jesus Christ, Anna, call the fire department." Then he was down the hall, moving faster than he realized his legs would allow, and on the phone bellowing out about his hay being afire.

The smoke rose up and drifted steadily toward his house on the wind, blotting out the stars like the permanent marker he used down at the station to ink out people's social security numbers from back when they accepted such things as identification. He could barely see the flames through the smoke, but when they did leap, they were as he always imagined fire to be: out of control.

The volunteer fire department showed up with one truck full of water, the other empty. An argument ensued about whose responsibility it had been to fill the second truck. Finally, the chief stepped in and said water wouldn't do any good anyhow.

"Look at it," he said. "Every time we douse it, it rears right back up again. Them bales is wound too tight."

Harold thought how he had prided himself on being able to wind a bale tighter than most others, even with his baler and its rusted sides and worn belts. He'd always thought that keeping the bale tight would make it stay fresh over the winter. He remembered when people burned straw twisted into tight knots for heat, back when coal was a luxury. He had played right into the fire's hands.

The chief called a neighbor who had a front-end loader with a hay fork attachment. He came and lifted the blazing bales of hay, one by one, and set them out in the forty acres across from Harold's house. Forty. Fifty. Sixty. Seventy. Eighty-four bales they took out of a pen of just over 120.

Harold stayed up watching the bales burn. They lit the field up, the color orange arranged across it in dimples between stretches of black deeper than shadows, like a flock of pagan rituals spread out in front of him. And the smoke rose up and made the sky black.

Harold was in the station before 7 a.m. the next morning. The sun had been up for a while. He had watched it rise and shine on the front forty, the bales still smoldering. Frosty wasn't in until 8 a.m., and Harold needed some distractions, so he turned on the little television and watched an early morning news show, which didn't interest him much. They jumped from topic to topic like confused fleas. One minute, politics. The next, how to make your own wedding dress. Then where to go on vacation. If to go on vacation. He switched it off at 7:45 a.m., got up from his desk, and opened the bay doors. He turned on a few machines, including an older computer he tried to use daily to make it appear as if his business was cutting edge. He brewed a pot of coffee and sat down behind the desk again to wait for Frosty. When the coffee was done, he was still waiting. Frosty was a little late, which wasn't normal, but not unusual either. Harold, however, wanted him there. Needed him. He came in at 8:20 a.m., his uniform hanging loose off his lanky bones like clothes picked up at the Salvation Army.

"Sorry I'm late," he said, pulling up a chair. He took the coffee and poured it into a mug that read *FROSTY'S MUG* in stenciled lettering. He had been employed at the garage for nearly fifteen years, had brought the mug with him when he started and, to Harold's knowledge, had never washed it.

"Fine by me," Harold said. "Ain't much to tell anyhow."

"Never is," Frosty said, half laughing.

"'Cept I lost over half my hay last night," Harold said. He leaned back in his chair and pulled his hand through his starchy hair, stroked his beard that he'd stopped trimming since Anna died.

"Lost it?" Frosty asked.

"Lost it," Harold said.

"Well, where'd you put it?"

"Didn't put it no place," Harold said. "It burned up."

"Burnt up?" Frosty asked. He put his coffee down. "Well, I'll be damned. You know, I've heard of that kind of thing happening in a corn bin, but inside a bale of hay? Never heard of such a thing."

"They don't think it was spontaneous," Harold said. "They came back out late last night. Well, early this morning, I suppose, and looked it over. Said it was arson. Said they found residue."

"Residue of what?"

"Don't know," Harold said. "Gasoline I imagine. What else gonna make it burn like that? Smoke blacker than about anything."

"Somebody burnt up your hay?"

"Sure seems like it," Harold said.

"Well, who was it?"

"Now how am I supposed to know that?"

"Don't know," Frosty said. "Thought you might have an inkling."

"I do," Harold said. "But I ain't suppose to talk about it none."

"No?"

"No. Sheriff and the fire chief want to keep it quiet. There'll be an investigation, I suppose."

"Yeah," Frosty said. "That makes sense." He picked up his coffee mug again and raised it to his lips. From behind the mug he said, "Oh, wanted to tell you that Donna is stopping by today. Said she's got the front end of her Wrangler all outta whack. Told her I'd take a look."

"You do realize," Harold said, "that she's thirty-six and you're fifty-seven?"

"Yeah, I figured that," Frosty said.

"You also realize we've got a full plate today?"

"Yeah, I figured that, too."

"So, what you got to say for yourself, then?"

Frosty stood a minute, thinking.

"I'll work on her on my lunch," he said finally. Harold grumbled. He didn't approve, of course. Frosty was much too old for the woman, much too old. They looked like a pair of miscreants walking around together, sauntering into the local bar where they had met three months ago, dawdling over a milkshake with two straws in it at the Dairy Freeze, falling all over each other at church softball league night. As if Frosty were some kind of kid. As if she were old enough to understand anything about being old in the first place.

Harold shrugged. "Do what you want, but don't let Melvin's Pontiac sit another day. I ain't telling him again the part is backordered."

"So, what else is on the board today?" Frosty asked.

They went over the list. A few oil changes. Two tune-ups. A tire rotation. A flat to fix; that was first. And then Bill Wallace intended to bring his tractor in to have it greased. Frosty set to work on the flat. Harold went to find the grease gun that worked with the fittings on Wallace's tractor. The day danced forward, and Harold felt much more comfortable when the work day demanded to lead.

Donna Maytree had Native American blood in her, and every drop of it, as thin as it was, oozed out of her silk-like black hair that spilled down her back and over her shoulders.

The blood shone from her hazel eyes and glistened through her warm cocoa skin. She was thirty-six, but she didn't look it. Her strong legs sculpted her jeans. She walked in as if she owned places, and most places didn't mind.

It was noon, and the sun was warmer than usual. Harold sat at his desk, waiting on his Hungry Man dinner in the microwave behind him. Frosty had finished the Pontiac, and Harold had called Melvin Harris to let him know the car was ready.

"'Bout damn time," Melvin had said. Harold hadn't said anything. He had been lying to the man for two days, the part for his car sitting in a box on his desk, staring back at him as he spoke into the phone. But now the part was on the car, and things could move forward, until, of course, Donna Maytree walked in and disrupted everything. She was, for all Harold could surmise, a little like a tidal wave.

"Hey, Sugar," she called to Frosty, who leapt out from under the hood of a Ford F-150; he was changing the oil. Some tools clanged on the floor, and Harold swore under his breath. "Come on over here and give me some lovin'."

They preceded to give each other lovin' right there in the bay near the big drum of used oil that was more than half full. They kept at it until Harold gave a little cough and turned to the microwave, which made his old chair creak. He opened and slammed the microwave door. They stopped, but then they were in front of his desk, standing before him like two children waiting for their punishment.

"Hey Harold," Donna said.

"Donna," he said, peeling back the plastic on the microwave dinner. The steam rose up and burned his arm a little.

Donna turned to Frosty. "You told him yet?"

"Naw," Frosty said. "I ain't told him."

"Well, shit, Forrest. When you gonna tell him?"

"Tell me what?" Harold interrupted.

Frosty scratched the back of his neck. The same way he did when he wanted a day off.

"Well, it's like this," he started.

"We're gettin' married," Donna said with a flat voice.

Harold leaned back in his chair.

"Good for you," he said.

"You approve?" Frosty asked.

"Christ, Frosty, I ain't your father."

"I suppose," he said. "But it'd be nice if you'd approve. Seein' how I was gonna ask you to be in the wedding and all. Best man, you know?"

"Oh," Donna said, "and we're movin' to St. Louis."

"Movin'?" Harold asked. Frosty didn't say anything. He was still scratching the back of his neck. Donna put a hand on her hip, got defensive.

"There's not a thing to do about it," she said. "Our mind is made up."

"I can see that," Harold said. "I'm just wonderin' about him." He jabbed his finger at Frosty. "What about you? You movin'?"

"I just said we're movin'," Donna said.

"I heard ya," Harold scoffed. "I want to hear him."

"Yeah," Frosty said, defeated. "Yeah, I'm movin'."

Harold took a plastic fork from his desk and stabbed into the gray mass of fake mashed potatoes and rubbery Salisbury steak.

"Damn you," he said then. "Damn your eyes anyway. Where I gonna get me a good person for here? You think any of these little farts around here can change a goddamn tire, much less replace a carburetor? What do you think's gonna happen to this place?" He threw the fork across the room. Some of the gravy flung off and went into Donna's hair. Frosty slinked back a bit.

"And married. Married?" He turned to Donna. "You're barely old enough to shit alone. And you," he said to Frosty, "got two feet sticking out of the ground with all the bacon and shit you eat. Hotdamnit, you've made me cuss." Harold found himself standing, the two of them backing away, and he sat down.

"You're just jealous," Donna said, but she turned away when Harold looked up. With Frosty's hand in hers, she led him out of the garage. They knocked the old lug wrench off a counter as they fumbled their way outside. Harold heard the doors on her Wrangler shut with a soft muffle, as if they were trying to sneak away, and the gravel crunched under the tires until they hit the pavement. Harold went back to his potatoes, stirring them with the gravy until they turned into a gray mush. He found another fork and cut the Salisbury steak in half and tossed one half out the window behind him where a mutt covered in mange came and began gnawing at it. He kept an ear out for the Wrangler, hoping it would return. He called Frosty's place after he ate and listened to the buzzer burr at him, remembering how Frosty had said he'd never buy an answering machine after all the problems they'd had with the one at the station. He kept listening, hoping for some sound, hoping to hear something other than the lug wrench's ringing clang.

When Harold pulled into his driveway, he found the sheriff's car waiting for him. The whole way home, he was looking forward to just relaxing on the front porch, smoking his pipe, maybe drinking some iced tea. He couldn't shake the day off him. Even while he finished some of the day's work, which he did half-heartedly, he thought of the look on Frosty's face when he'd snapped, how the man had backed away like a frightened dog. He had tried Frosty's number twice more with no luck and thought to himself that he'd call later when Frosty would surely be home; that thought made him feel better.

The sheriff was on his porch, leaning against one of the posts, chewing tobacco, and spitting it on Harold's lawn. He came out to where Harold parked his truck and stood next to the door so Harold couldn't open it. He kept looking out toward the front forty where the bales had burned down to piles of black ash. Some of them still smoked.

"Damn shame," the sheriff said.

"Sure is," Harold said. "Guess there's worse, though."

"Well," the sheriff said, "we know who it was. I'm gonna go get him now. You want to come along?"

Harold moved around in his seat. "That normal?" he asked.

"No," the sheriff said. "Just thought I'd ask. Informal like and all."

"I've been asked and told a lot today," Harold said.

"That so?"

Harold nodded. The sheriff spit, and some of the juice got on Harold's truck.

"I'll go with you," Harold said. He thought of Frosty being pulled out to that woman's Jeep Wrangler. It made him boil a little, smolder, as if he were an old fire with just a little left in him. "I'd like to see it myself."

They rode in the sheriff's car. Harold studied all the gadgets and gizmos adorning the dashboard. The computer, which looked more advanced than the one at the garage, the radio, the scanner, the radar gun. Tools of the trade, and Harold wondered if other people looked over his garage with the same kind of wonderment. Probably not.

The sheriff drove slowly, dodging the mud holes and the places where the road had washboarded. He finally turned in at a drive that led back through a stand of old oaks and maples with long trunks and high branches. The sun came through the trees, lancing in under their leaves, making slants of light that came in the sheriff's window and made a glare. At the end of the drive were three trailers, two of them obviously not habitable. All three had rust on the sides, holes near their base. There were four or five dogs roaming around, all mangy but apparently well-fed. None of the dogs barked when they got out. Behind the trailers there was a long, low barn that looked like an old chicken coop. It had been painted red at one point, but the paint was nearly gone now. Only flecks remained. The barn sat near the edge of the clearing, right up against the woods. The sheriff opened his door. "Look," he said, "we're gonna get this done, and then I'm gonna check out that barn out back. Just have a look around."

Harold waited in the car. He rolled the window down and could smell the stink of dirty living. He wondered if they had running water. They lived so close to him, just down the road, not even two miles, even closer to the Handerhams, and here they were, living like lost nomads.

The sheriff went up and pounded on the door. A lady answered. She wore a long dress that covered her slender frame in bright flowers: blue, pink, orange, red, and purple. Her hair was tied up behind her head, and Harold was close enough to see that she looked old, with lines all over her face. The sheriff spoke a few words to her, and she began shaking her head. Harold could hear her saying, "No. No, he ain't." And then the sheriff had her by the arms and began pulling her out the door. He yanked her then, flinging her around, her thin body toppling over and rolling down the rickety wooden steps, landing in a small lump. The sheriff went into the trailer and came out with a young boy, his hands bound behind him. He wrestled the boy past the frail woman, who reached out and grabbed the boy around the ankles.

"You ain't takin' him," she shouted, holding on. And Harold leaned back in his seat, pressed back so his spine straightened into the cushions as the sheriff drug both of them, boy in hand, woman grasping at his ankles, across the

dirt and gravel lot to where the car was parked. He opened
the back door and went to where the mother had hold of
the boy. He stepped down on her hand with his boot, and
she let out a wail and screamed, "No" as the boy was taken
from her and tossed in the backseat where he landed sideways
with a quiet puff of air. Harold wasn't sure if it was from
him or the seat.

"Well, that's done," the sheriff said. "I'm gonna take a
look around back now."

"Guess we could just get on," Harold said. "I've got my
cows to look at back home."

"Only be a minute," the sheriff said. "The man here's
got a record for distributing meth. He cooks it out back in
that barn, so we check it now and then. Just thought I'd take
a look in case I need to haul them all off."

Behind them, the woman sat in the gravel holding her
hand up to her chest.

"You ain't taking him," she said repeatedly, with less
conviction as she swayed back and forth.

"Is he here?" Harold asked.

"Yeah, he's inside, but don't worry about him. He knows
better. I've tangled with 'im a time or two."

The sheriff walked back toward the barn, and Harold
sat and listened to the boy wheeze in the backseat. He tried
to glance back to get a look, but he could only see the boy's
hair, back, and feet. The hair was filled with bits of straw
and covered in dirt. He was trying to look at the boy when
the mother came through his window, grabbing at his shirt,
screeching at him.

"You let him go, you dirty bastard," she screamed. "Get
him outta here." She clawed at him, raking her fingernails
across his face. Harold fought back, pushing the woman
until she was out of the car and then rolling up the window.
She slammed her fists on the glass.

"Do you know what I've lost?" she shouted at him,

muffled through the glass. "Do you know? You piece of shit. Do you know?"

The sheriff came running from behind the house. He grabbed the woman from behind and lifted her, kicking and screaming, and carried her back to the house where he gently set her down on the porch. He put a hand on her shoulder and spoke to her, and then Harold saw the man appear in the doorway in a cutoff T-shirt and no pants. Harold rolled the window back down.

"Maggie," the man said, "ain't nothing to do about it. Come on in here."

"You're a chickenshit," she said.

"They got a right to do whatever they're doing," he said to her. "Come on in before they do it to you, too."

She got up then, but Harold could tell from her face that the fight wasn't out of her yet. The sheriff came back to the car. The boy sat up in the backseat and watched out the window with a blank stare. Harold turned around and looked him in the face. He could see the boy's jawbone, could see where the boy's eyes had sunken in.

"You all right back there?" Harold asked. But the boy didn't say anything. He lay back down in the seat. "You know what's going on?" Still nothing. "They say you lit some hay afire. You do that?"

The boy sat up. There were tears in his eyes.

The sheriff got back in the car and began to back up. From the driveway, the mother threw rocks at the car. One hit the windshield.

"I really should just take her in," the sheriff said.

"Let it be," Harold said.

The sheriff kept backing up until he found a place to turn the car around. The rocks hit the back windshield for a moment until the car was out of her range, and they pulled out onto the main gravel road and headed for Harold's house.

Harold kept glancing back at the boy.

"He don't look like an arsonist," Harold said. "Besides he's only a boy."

"They never do look like anything they've done," the sheriff said. "And that don't matter much." The sheriff pulled into Harold's driveway. "Here you go. Guess there was some vindication in that. Hope there was anyway."

"You know," Harold said, getting out of the car, "Frosty's leaving the garage. Don't know where I'll get the help I need to keep it going."

"Guess there's a little perspective in that," the sheriff said.

Harold walked up the drive to his porch. From there he could see the boy in the backseat, still leaning against the window. Behind the car were the bales of hay he'd lost with the sun going down behind them and the sky turning pink again. He went inside and brought a glass of iced tea out to the porch. When he came back, he saw Jacob Handerham again, walking down in the ditch, smoking a cigarette, flicking the ashes down on the ground. He was headed home to his father and their way of doing things. The sheriff's car, still visible, stirred up dust that hovered off the road, soft as a pillow, in the dwindling light.

The cold front that blew in the night before brought the year's first frost with it. When Harold woke the next morning, just as the sun's light came through the low gray clouds, he saw the ground dusted white, the piles of ashen hay now piles of white glistening in the low light. It was rather beautiful and calm, and Harold couldn't help but think of Frosty, waking up with Donna by him, his arm reaching out to her, the stiffness in his neck giving way as he touched her back and she slid closer to him. Same as he and Anna used to do on cold mornings when they were young.

He brewed coffee at home, for the smell more than

anything, and hung around the house picking up things he'd left lying around for too long until almost 8:30. Then he went out to his truck, climbed in, and drove down the drive. At the road where he should have turned right, he turned left and drove over the washboard sections, his truck bouncing from side to side. He drove past the Handerham's and on to the little road that led back through the trees to the heap of a trailer and the trash-filled yard. He got out and patted the dog that came up to him. He thought it odd that the dogs were so docile, what with the man being a convicted drug dealer and all. He went up to the door and knocked. The sound was muffled by the insulated door. It opened, which he didn't expect, and Harold found himself standing in front of the man he'd seen the day before.

"Morning," the man said. "Help you?"

"Yeah," Harold said, reaching his hand around behind his neck. He began scratching before he realized what he was doing and snatched his hand back to his side. "I'm Harold Dentamore. I live up the road a ways."

"Dentamore?" the man said. "You own that station up on the highway?"

"That's right," Harold said.

"Yeah, I thought I knowed you. Been there a few times. Had the oil changed in my Caddy."

Harold didn't remember the man. It frustrated him more that he didn't remember the car. He hadn't worked on many Cadillacs in his time. He figured the man was lying.

"Well," Harold said, "I meant to talk to you yesterday."

"Yesterday?"

"Yeah," Harold said, stepping back a bit, almost falling off the top step. "Yesterday. I was here. With the sheriff. Your wife, she threw rocks at us."

"Oh, all that shit. She ain't my wife. She just lives here with me and my boy. Besides, she's gone anyhow. Addict was all she was. Plum through."

"Your boy?"

"Yessir. My boy. They hauled him off yesterday. Did you say you was here?"

"Yes, I did."

"Didn't see you. Saw that son of a bitch Langer, but not you. Where was you?"

"I was in the car," Harold said. He was scratching the back of his neck again.

"Well," the man said. "You the law?"

"No," Harold said. "I just run a station." He put his hand in his pocket. The move made the man's eyes go down, stare at his hand, and jump a little. "Look," Harold said, "about your boy. They said that he burnt up my hay down the road a ways."

"Did they?"

"Sure they did. Why do you think they came and got him?"

"Cause of who he is," the man said. "Don't matter much of none if he done it or not when he's my kin. He knows all about that."

Harold thought about the boy's face in the backseat, about the tears he'd seen, and how calm the boy had been.

"I don't think he did it," Harold said. "I'd like the two of us to go on in to town and clear this all up right now. Your boy ought to be home."

"I ain't goin' nowhere near that place," the man said. "Minute they see me, I'll be right in there with him."

"I don't see how we can make this right if you don't come along," Harold said.

"Ain't no right to it," the man said. "Get me a pen."

"How's that?"

"A pen," the man said. "I'll write down you can take him out, into custody, you know? And they'll let him go on that."

"That legal?"

"Mostly," the man said. "They done it before."

Harold reached in his shirt pocket and pulled out a stubby pencil he kept there for when he needed to measure something. The man wrote upright on the open door. He handed Harold the note, and Harold felt small in front of him. He was calm, the man, as calm as frost freezing.

At the police station, Harold gave the note to the sheriff. The boy wasn't in a cell. He was sitting on a couch in the lobby. He wasn't chained or cuffed or anything. He was just sitting there, told to stay.

"Juvee couldn't get him last night," the sheriff said. "I had to take him to my place. Edith threw a shit fit, but he was fine there on the living room floor. Didn't hurt a thing, and Edith made him some oatmeal this morning so he shouldn't be too hungry."

Harold nodded.

"Where you gonna take him? Back there?"

Harold nodded again.

The boy followed Harold out to the truck and climbed in. They drove down Main Street, past the MFA Feed Store where Harold saw some people he knew. They watched him drive by with the boy in the front seat. He knew they'd talk about it later, probably with their feet propped up against the cast iron stove. They'd speculate on what was going on, and they'd come to their own conclusions, with their feet still propped up. There wasn't a one of them who ever knocked on a trailer door. Not a one of them in any of their godforsaken lives. He drove past them without a customary wave that people in Wynott gave to others they didn't even know. He kept driving out of town, toward home. Then he veered off, took a familiar left, and drove into the station's small parking lot.

He told the boy to come in, and they sat down together, the boy across from Harold who sat at his desk. He turned on the computer.

"I know it ain't much," Harold said. "But it's about all I got left."

The boy looked around. When he turned his head, Harold could see little scars near his ears where it looked like someone with long fingernails had grabbed his head and dug in through the skin.

"You want to work here?" Harold said. The boy didn't say anything. "You don't say much. That's fine by me. I don't say much either. Let's do this. You want to work here, you go out there in the bay and just tidy up a little bit. You do that, and I'll know you want to stay. I'll pay you a fair wage for a boy your age, and you can work here. I'll pick you up every morning. As long as it's fine with your old man."

The boy didn't acknowledge him. He just sat there.

The day wore on. Harold moved around the bay, around the garage, doing odd jobs, filling out paperwork Frosty had left on the clipboard. The phone didn't ring. Frosty didn't call. Harold imagined him balled up in the front seat of a Jeep Wrangler riding north toward St. Louis, wedding bells ringing in his dreams.

It was noon. Harold went back to his desk and found the boy still sitting there. He sat down opposite the boy, opened the little refrigerator, and pulled out a Hungry Man dinner of turkey and mashed potatoes. He put it in the microwave and punched the timer buttons. The boy stared at the food with hungry dog eyes.

"You can have some," Harold said. The timer went off, and he turned around to get the food. When he turned back, the boy was gone. Harold stood up and looked to see if he'd ducked down on the floor. He saw him then, out in the bay. The boy moved around for a moment, looking at the different machines, running his hands over them, touching the tools. He went over to a car that was on the lift from where Frosty had left it the day before and reached up and touched its underbelly, soft, like he was touching an infant. He came back toward Harold's desk, his face still blank. The mangy dog came in, probably looking for his customary handout. He sat next to the boy who knelt down and began rubbing the dog's head. The boy leaned away from the dog, picked up the lug wrench from where it had fallen, and gently placed it back on the counter.

Best Road Yet

It was wrong what they were doing, forcing an old man to travel so far in the Taurus's cramped backseat. They tried to get him to sit up front, but it didn't work. He kept opening the door, so they finally left him in the back where childproof locks kept him in. Ted drove with Arnez in the passenger seat. A map lay between them, the route outlined in pink highlighter. They ate peanuts and potato chips and didn't stop. The crumbs gathered in the seat creases. The old man snored as his white, dry tongue dangled out, steadied by his chapped lips. The car smelled of stale, wet clothes.

They went through Big Cabin and paid for the toll road, trying to recognize the thin, weak-looking trees, huddled in groups. Lower stood scraggly bushes with short branches full of thorns. It all pulsated in the heat lines, danced in the stiff Oklahoma wind, blowing east in waves that pushed the car an inch or more with each gust.

There had been talk of backing out, turning the car around, and returning to Missouri.

"You want me to drive?" Arnez asked.

"No," Ted said. "Relax. You drive tomorrow. Tomorrow will be the long day."

Arnez leaned his seat back so it hit the old man's knees.

"Easy," Ted said.

"It's all right," Arnez said. "He's asleep anyway. You know we could've taken him up to Laramie. He has family there, too."

"Who?" Ted asked.

"I don't know." Arnez pulled out a cigarette, stuck it in his mouth. It muffled his speech. He closed his eyes and said, "It would've been on the way for me."

"You talk too easy," Ted said.

"I'm a realist."

"Sure you are."

"In Montana," Arnez said, waving his cigarette, "you have to be."

Ted knew about the woman Arnez lived with who owned a ranch with an ocean-wide sky as blue as frostbite.

"Have you talked to that Potts girl lately?" Arnez asked.

"I haven't seen her," Ted said.

"Give her a call when we get back. It'll be good for you."

"It'll be great."

"You shouldn't be like that. Call her up," Arnez said. "It'll be time to get on with things, Teddy. That's what we're doing here. We're making things easier on everyone."

"I've only talked to her twice. Once at a funeral."

They had a misunderstanding deep as the 7-11 Big Gulp held between Arnez's thighs. Ted recalled a sugar-coated childhood in flashes, framed and faded at the old house in Wynott. Because Arnez lived far away, Ted could think, *Sure, that's how it was,* when he stared at the photographs of them with their arms draped around each other. Arnez had never done Ted any favors.

He had realized on a Saturday three months ago that life had become more folded like a wrinkled map than he'd ever imagined. There were only a few solutions for breaking free from a loop like that, a road that twisted and laid right back onto itself. He started planning. The mockingbird rested in the maple tree out front. Ted stretched out on the front porch, his body sore from a night of tossing in and out of sleep. The old man called out names of long-dead relatives and words that sounded backwards. Ted was sure there were others like himself somewhere—people who had nothing to lose—but he didn't know any of them. He didn't really know anyone. He knew things like the angles of cracks in the plaster walls, the sound of pipes squawking when the water came on in the upstairs bathroom, and which floorboards creaked loud enough to wake the old man.

"Surely," he'd said to Arnez on the phone later that evening, "there's a way out of this. Don't you have money? For a home?" A buzz rang in his ear, the heavy weight of Montana snow resting on the line, dragging it down.

Arnez said his money was all tied up, so he couldn't get to it.

The old man came in the room and stood behind Ted. "Who's it?" he asked.

"Arnez," Ted said.

"Who?"

"Arnez."

"Who's it?"

Ted turned back to the phone. "Gotta be a way," he said. "Ask Jeanie for the money. She's got money. We could borrow it together." He didn't bother to whisper or cover the phone. He felt he could turn around and look in the old man's eyes, tell him they were getting rid of him, an old dog never worth much in the first place.

More buzz. Arnez said things weren't good with Jeanie.

"Ask her to help," Ted said.

Now, as the sun bore down on them from the West, stretching out the shadows of the stocky Oklahoma trees, the old man only made sleeping sounds in the backseat, turning over and occasionally moving around. Ted glanced back. In the rearview mirror, he saw how low the old man's eyes sank, how the skin under them drooped and shadowed. The sky framed the low, long horizon where a green tint rose up off the ground—the place where the grass turned the sky green, an illusion just above the stretched-out road. It was a lot to see.

On the toll road, the rhythmic bumps disappeared and only a smooth whine remained. The old man lifted himself and peered out the rear window. His long, thin hair swept over his shoulders in greasy strands. Arnez looked more like him than Ted did. Ted had his mother's eyes, and every time he glanced back, he caught an accusing look from her, settled in those eyes set wide apart by a broad nose. He squinted, scrunched his face so the folds of skin altered his reflection into something he could stand.

"Good road," the old man said.

"It is," Ted said. "I've never driven in Oklahoma before."

"You've never driven anywhere before," Arnez said.

The old man looked at both of them with his arms up over the two seats so the sweat rings under his arms showed.

"Are you hot back there?" Ted asked.

"No," the old man said. "Yes," he said then. Ted turned up the air conditioning.

Arnez said, "That'll hurt the gas mileage."

"Let it," Ted said. "He should at least be comfortable. Don't you think?"

For a while they rode that way, with the air blasting over them, making Ted's skin bumpy. They passed trucks, and the old man recited the states where they originated. He read the billboards and the road signs out loud. Arnez told him to keep quiet.

"It's good for him," Ted said. "It helps keep his mind sharp."

"Annoying as hell," Arnez said. "Really, Teddy, I don't know how you've put up with him."

"Once you get into a rhythm, anything's easy," Ted said.

Eighteen-wheel trucks surrounded the car and blocked out the road signs. Their silver grills glinted in the sun, grinning at the little Taurus. Ted missed an exit with a gas station and turned around. Through all of this, the old man slept in the backseat with his legs propped up against the window, revealing his dirty socks.

The road turned due south in Oklahoma City, and they moved across traffic lanes. Low and off the road, they found a motel with rotting edges and grass growing through cracks in the concrete parking lot. Inside, Ted gave his credit card to a chunky old woman who kept incense burning in the office behind the counter. The smell reminded him of church: spiced wood and smoke floating over his head.

"Just one room?" the woman asked, her voice creaky, different from the soft, plucky Chinese music drifting in with the incense. She wore a kimono wrapped tightly around her belly. Her folds showed.

Ted thought of his father's first business partner, an Oriental man, short with a prematurely bald head and narrow eyes. Ted never trusted those eyes, even when he was old enough to know they were genetic. But the man's wife. Graceful. Smooth as the silk she wore. Her face soft like fresh snow in the sun. The partners would meet on Saturdays, strolling around the back lawn, discussing how to sell more vacuum cleaners. The Oriental man with his arms always moving. Ted's father's hands shoved deep in khaki pockets. They'd stop occasionally and share a drink from a flask.

The women waited at the bay window with coffee cups. His mother's flowers trembled just beyond the panes, and the Oriental's wife never spoke. *No English*, she could say. She would gesture with her small hands, her fingers moving like the drifting spider webs caught on the marigolds. All the time, Ted watched the Oriental man's wife move and fell in love with the way her face matched her gestures. How her eyes would soften, shoulders relax, and fingers slow when his mother mentioned the problems with Arnez or, sometimes, with Ted's father. No words in return, a one-way street, an understanding of the voice tone of such things.

"Just one," Ted said to the kimono lady. "Do you have one with a sofa?"

"No," she said.

"All right, just one then. Two beds. Do you have breakfast?"

"Nope," she said. "There's a Denny's just down the road."

"Is there an IHOP close?"

"Ten miles or so," she said. She raked the credit card copy machine over his card. It made a grating sound. "Check out at ten."

He found Arnez standing against the passenger door.

"No sofas," Ted said.

"Hell," Arnez said. "We oughta move on down the road."

"We're worn out," Ted said. "I'll sleep on the floor. Help me get him out of the car."

They opened the back door and found the old man bent double in the backseat. His knees pulled up near his chest. He wheezed and coughed as they pulled on his legs and arms, yanking him as if he were being born out of the car.

"Come on, Dad," Ted kept saying. "Come on. It's time to get out."

"I don't think we can get him out of there without hurting him," Arnez said. He reached in and grabbed the old man by the wrist and pulled hard. Ted heard a pop.

"What are you doing?" Ted said, going for Arnez's arm.

Arnez pulled again.

The old man screamed, "They're killing me, Beth! They're trying to kill me!"

Arnez hissed through his teeth, "Get out of there."

Then the old man slid onto the pavement, as if Arnez had found the right angle to pry him out. He sat on the cooling concrete, looking around, his wrist clutched close to his chest.

"Let me see that arm," Arnez said. He held it up and moved it around. "Nothing broken." Ted could see Arnez's hand outlined in purple around the old man's wrist.

"Look what you did," he said. He kneeled down and took the old man's hand in his, watching the skin slide as he turned the wrist over gently to get a better look at the dark bruise.

"He's tired," Arnez said. He lit another cigarette. "Let's take him inside. You got a smoking room, didn't you?"

"I don't know. Look at the card."

Arnez looked. "Yep," he said. "Smoking for sure. Good job, Teddy. You done all right."

Bright lights blinked all up and down the street. Fast food joints. Bowling alleys. More hotels lined up like barns. Flashing arrows promising the best steak, the best lobster. A strip club. The Interstate roared behind them with the constant cry of asphalt. They carried the old man in, one son on each arm.

The room had a dank feel, as if it hadn't been cleaned in a while. It smelled of tired workers, sweat, and weak deodorant. Arnez dropped the old man on the bed and went out. He came back with a bottle of Evan Williams. He unwrapped the motel plastic cups.

"No damn ice machine," he said. He poured two glasses.

Ted took one and drank it. He had trouble with his drinking now, hitting it twice a week when a year ago he was down to nil. The Evan Williams stung his throat like a needle prick.

"The woman at the desk was wearing a kimono," Ted said.

"No shit?"

"Like the wife of that partner Dad had. What was her name?"

"Kim."

"Right," Ted said. "I remember her."

"Yeah," Arnez said. "Me, too. You know, they had a thing." He pointed at the old man with the bottle. "About four years."

"When?" Ted asked.

"Just before he met the other one," Arnez said. "You know she was a mail-order bride? Hated it here. That's what Mom said."

Ted thought of Beth Dobson, the "other one," her thin legs and long arms, and her son, Earl. Beth made cookies for them and dressed her porch with pumpkins, square bales, and mums in October, lights at Christmas, and bright flags in July. Ted knew about Kim and Beth, but before Ted could fathom imperfections in their parents, Arnez swallowed them like he did Evan Williams now, in long, bubbly gulps.

"I was thinking," Arnez said, "about that time he came and got us in the woods."

The old man slept on the bed—his body frail and small in the lamplight.

"I remember that," Ted said.

"I think that's the last good thing I remember about him," Arnez said. "I don't remember much but him coming through the trees, all dark and tall."

"With the sun behind him," Ted said. "I dream it sometimes."

"God," Arnez said, "you were just a kid."

"Sometimes," Ted said, "I think he should've just left us out there."

Arnez went over to the bed. He stood over the old man, looking down.

"You know how many times I've stood right here?" he said. "Just thinking about covering his face with a pillow?"

And Ted knew why. It had been a Monday. Their father and mother were driving home from somewhere. That night etched in Ted's mind like the burn scars on Arnez's arm. Their father came home; their mother didn't. He was twelve then.

"That's why I'm here," Arnez said. "So what about you?"

Ted said nothing. He took another pull on the whiskey.

"There's thousands of people like you," Arnez said. "Dangling on the end of your rope, but not all of them cut loose. People who take their old parents in, stuff them in some corner room to clean up their shit. Role reversal and all that. They don't all lose it, Teddy. They don't call their brothers up and say, 'Let's take him to Texas.' So what happened to you?"

Ted thought of Marie Potts, of seeing her in the parking lot outside the IHOP where he used to take the old man day in and day out because the routine was all that mattered. He thought about her long legs and her back, how her shoulders made little creases in her shirt when she bent over to pull weeds from a flowerbed.

"That's what I thought," Arnez said. "Same as always. You don't have a clue."

But Ted did. He did have a clue. The old man began to snore on the nearby bed. On the table were brochures from nightclubs in Oklahoma City, and Ted had a clear clue. All that blue he'd seen earlier, as they whistled through Oklahoma, seemed incredibly small compared to what he could see now. The snoring didn't bother him. In fact, he

couldn't even hear it. He couldn't hear Arnez cuss at him
when he didn't answer. He could hear wind. Wind blowing
cleanly through maple trees, grabbing the scent of sap, lofting
pollen right into his bedroom window on the second floor
of *his* home in Wynott—a window that had been shut for
ten years.

They drank a few more glasses. Ted lay down on the
hard floor and breathed in the musty smell of dust.

Arnez drove the next day. He stopped at a McDonald's
and ordered everyone coffee and sausage biscuits.

"This is not good," Ted said. He tossed the greasy wrapper
on the dashboard. "Dad needs his routine. We need to go to
IHOP."

"It'll be fine," Arnez said. "Look at him. He's fine."

The old man lay across the backseat, chewed on his food,
and sipped his coffee.

"You don't understand," Ted said. "It's fine now, but it
won't be in an hour or so."

"Get over it. You need to fucking relax."

Ted laid his seat back and closed his eyes, trying to relax.
But all he could see was the old man sitting in a dusty upstairs
room in their Wynott home, shivering in the corner while
Ted tried to get him to stand up, tried to get him to take a
shower or a bath, and all of this because they had broken
the routine. Ted had overslept.

Wide fields opened up around them with motionless
oil rigs among grazing cattle staring beyond the fences.
All of it swirled by as Arnez pressed the accelerator down
and pushed the car up to eighty-five. The engine quivered
and then began to buzz. The road turned rougher, and
Arnez moved over to the passing lane to find smoother
sailing.

"Not a very good road," he said, but Ted was asleep, and

the old man had occupied himself by swirling his unfinished coffee with his finger.

Then the old man said, "When we gonna get some pancakes?"

Arnez looked in the rearview. The old man was up, leaning forward toward the front seat.

"Not today," Arnez said into the mirror.

"When?"

"Not today. No pancakes today. We're making time here."

The old man sat back and put a hand on his head. He looked as if he were trying to come up with an answer to a difficult question. His face squeezed together; his eyes narrowed.

"When?" he asked again.

"Not today," Arnez said, slower this time.

The old man rotated himself around so he could lean back against the door. He began unbuttoning his shirt and sweating.

"Calm down back there," Arnez said. "Relax."

The old man undid his pants. He pissed on the backseat.

"Hey," Arnez shouted. "Hey, there. Stop that shit."

The car's sudden jerk woke Ted.

"What did you do?" he asked.

Arnez slowed the car and pulled onto the shoulder.

"Goddamnit," Arnez said. "The fucking car."

He got out and went around to the side where the old man leaned against the door.

"It's all right," Ted said. "We'll go."

The old man whimpered.

Arnez yanked the door open. "Get out of there," he said. He grabbed the old man by his shoulders, jerked him out, and threw him on the ground. The old man's pants bunched around his ankles. His stained underwear hung loosely around his waist, weighted in the back.

"Oh, Jesus," Arnez said. "Jesus. Shit."

He took the old man's shirt and began wiping the seat with it.

"You dirty old fuck," Arnez said. He came at the old man and hit him with the shirt. Cars went by on the Interstate. Diesels passed and brought wind that nearly knocked them down. Arnez dropped the shirt.

The old man lay on the ground. His eyes were wide. His hair tangled and wet with sweat. A little blood rolled from his lip where he'd bitten through it.

Arnez got back in the car and sat there with the engine running, the heat rising off the highway. Sweat ran down his neck and stained his collar. Little beads of it hung on his pointed chin and mustache, dangling just above his lips. Ted stood at the passenger window.

"All the phone calls," Arnez said. "All the time. Turning to me, looking for me to help. I'm helping, Teddy," he said. "I'm doing the best I can."

Ted looked south. They weren't even to Dallas yet and had at least five more hours on the road.

"I'll clean it up," he said. "Let's just get to the next town, and I'll figure out a way to clean him and the car."

Arnez sat staring down the highway that seemed to go on and on with no bends. Distant cars and semis were wavy lines of heat moving toward them.

Ted picked the old man off the road. He struggled to get up and whined when he put weight down on his right foot. Then Ted got in the front seat. He locked the doors, and Arnez pulled out onto the road.

"This isn't my car," Arnez said. "It's Jeanie's. You better get that goddamn smell out of here." He rolled the window down. "Do you know what she'll say? She'll leave me, and that's it, Teddy. I'll have to come back. Do you understand? If I bring this car back like this, if I fuck up again, ever, she's gone. I know it. You get that shit cleaned up."

"I will," Ted said. He rolled his own window down. In

the backseat, the old man's hair went wild in the wind. The strands stood up like points. They passed a road construction sign and hit the new pavement. The car evened out, and the hot, fresh air blew through in gusts.

"Good road," the old man said from the backseat.

Dallas grew out of suburbs and long strip malls. No skyscrapers yet, just miles and miles of flat buildings with tall signs. Four then five then six lanes of traffic. Lines of cars in front of and behind them. The old man stared out the window. He'd been quiet for the better part of an hour, only making noise when his stomach hurt. Arnez had stopped and bought him some peanut butter crackers to help him calm down, which had worked. But they had also given him indigestion.

Ted watched the signs go by, hoping for an IHOP and a way to avoid a repeat of that morning. Arnez reached in the glove compartment and pulled out a pint bottle of whiskey. The black label had faded.

"I've been saving this for some occasion," he said to Ted. "Thought I'd open it if I ever asked Jeanie to marry me. Don't think that'll happen now." He twisted the cap off and threw the bottle up to his lips. The brown liquid looked thick and sweet. He handed the bottle to Ted.

"Yeah?" Ted said, taking the whiskey as they used to do on the tailgate of Arnez's '58 Chevy up on Allegheny Hill in Wynott with the stars bright and the crickets all around.

"Here," he said, turning around, "drink this."

The old man took the bottle and put it up to his lips. He did it with ease, as he still did some things like combing his hair back with the slick hair gel he always used or splashing on his cologne or cutting his steak into tiny pieces. Those things grew into his muscles over time, just as lifting a bottle had, and now he lifted it again, his mouth and throat waiting.

"Not so much," Ted said, taking the bottle away.

"Lots of cars," the old man said. "Too many."

They passed the bottle between them, moving it along without saying anything. The whiskey drained down. Soon they all felt queasy from the heat and the wind blowing in. Arnez rolled up his window and turned on the A/C again. They felt the Taurus rock back and hesitate as the compressor kicked on. Arnez passed the bottle to Ted who drank and handed it to the old man who drank and handed it up to Arnez. They kept at it until the first bottle was gone.

"We've been out on the road too long," Arnez said. "Let's find a place to stop."

Arnez took the next exit, just as the city skyline dropped into view to their right. He pulled into a Holiday Inn and shut off the car.

"I'm going to get some cigarettes. Get the room, would ya Teddy?"

"What about Dad?" Ted asked.

"I'll take him. He can't do no harm in the gas station."

They pulled the old man out, and Arnez took him underneath the shoulders.

"We're going this way," he said.

They went across the parking lot with Arnez holding him under his arms. Ted watched them from the car until they'd gone behind a semi. The car still smelled. He had tried to remove the stains with little success. He went inside and found the hotel booked. The desk clerk put in a call to a few places down the road.

"I'm sorry," he said. "There's nothing until you get to Henderson."

"Where's that?"

"About two hundred miles," the clerk said.

Ted looked out the glass doors. Two hundred miles. He thought of the car's close quarters, the stench. The Taurus squatted in the parking lot. He looked past it. No sign of them. The parking lot shone a dull black under the streetlamps, like an old wet pair of patent leather shoes.

His brother and the old man came back. Ted could see the little red dot of Arnez's cigarette.

"Would you like me to call to Henderson?" the clerk asked.

"Yes," Ted said. "Call them."

Arnez kept driving. His face stern, eyes locked on the road. The old man sat in the backseat again, wheezing now.

"They didn't have *anything?*" Arnez said. "No broom closet? No bathroom? No couch in the lobby?"

"Nothing," Ted said.

"That's crazy. That guy was giving you shit." He had the other whiskey bottle out. "He probably saw him," he said, jabbing his thumb at the backseat, "and thought better of giving you a room."

"That's not what happened," Ted said.

"You know," Arnez said, "you're like a fucking woman. You whine and cry about everything." He had sobered and was mad again about the car's seat, the stench, and the heavy weight of what they were doing.

"Maybe I should drive," Ted said, trying to make an excuse. "You've had a lot to drink."

"No shit," Arnez said, but he didn't stop. Beneath them, the highway moaned. The car shook as if it didn't want anymore.

"You sure you can make it to Henderson?" Ted asked. He took the bottle and drank some, hoping to hold Arnez back a little.

"I'm going all the way," Arnez said. "We're taking care of things."

"That's tomorrow," Ted said. "We drive to Houston tomorrow."

"Hell with it," Arnez said. "This stops tonight. I've got

to get this fucking car cleaned, and I can't do that with him in here. So, it's tonight."

Ted leaned back. He felt sweat on his face. Air moved over him, cooling him and making his arms and wrists tingle. It was much, much too fast.

"We need to slow down," he said. "Think things over."

"I've been thinking for thirty-three years," Arnez said. "How 'bout you, Teddy. How long you been thinking?"

Ted thought of a ten-year-old Arnez, poised over their sleeping father, pillow in hand.

The old man leaned forward then. "You boys calm down up here," he said. "You're making a goddamn mess of things."

They stared forward, not looking at each other, watching the taillights.

Arnez pulled off into a rest area about sixty miles outside of Dallas. Ted sat in a trance in the passenger seat, not looking at anything. Arnez shook him.

"He needs to use the bathroom," Arnez said. "Get out and stretch your legs. I'm going to smoke."

Ted got out of the car. The heavy air grabbed him like a tight hand, and he felt his lungs contract. He pulled the old man out of the backseat and told him where they were and where they were going. He told the old man what was happening to him. Ted thought it was the least he could do. The old man seemed to understand.

Arnez went behind the car, smoking his cigarette, dropping the ashes into the wind blowing north from the Gulf. He listened as the two of them walked on into the rest area. A few cars sat quietly in parking spaces—their windows clear and dark. He could see people sleeping inside, their belongings piled high around them in the backseats or wrenched and tied on top of their SUVs.

Across the lot, the truckers were still awake, standing outside their rigs and talking to each other and to a few hookers. The parking lot light looked normal on their heavy shoulders. They passed a joint between them. Arnez could smell it from where he leaned. He flicked his cigarette and walked off toward the bathroom.

Ted pushed the steel door open and guided the old man in. The bathroom lights reflected off of everything: the steel stall doors, the stainless steel sinks, the steel urinals. Everything lit up. Smells of urine and disinfectant. Ted rested against one of the sinks, the metal cold through his pants. He could hear the old man in the stall trying to situate himself. He could feel the millions of pricks rising up his arm again.

"You okay in there?" Ted called. The old man grunted. Ted leaned down and peered under the stalls. He could see legs and lowered pants. Ted went to the stall door and jiggled it. It was locked. No one came in. The bathroom had old, pulsating lights.

"Almost done in there?" he said again.

Very alone. Calm. Ted began shaking a little, felt cold as he went to the bathroom door and opened it and walked out into the warm Texas air. He found Arnez waiting just outside, going through the brochures advertising restaurants in Houston and beaches in Galveston.

Ted shoved his hands in his pockets, lowered his shoulders. Arnez had the same look as the time they were lost in the woods. Defeated. Ted lifted his hand to his face and rubbed it but couldn't feel anything. His arms tingled around the wrists; his breath came in short gasps. Inside the bathroom, they could hear the old man banging around, probably trying to figure out the toilet paper dispenser.

"Hey," they heard him call. "Boys. Where you at?" His voice echoed off the metal sinks and urinals, bouncing away from them.

They had just moved out of town to the country, after their father had returned from running off with Beth Dobson. The two brothers had gone to the woods to hunt for snakes and were lost for the better part of the day. He'd come for them, a great man lumbering through the trees calling, *Boys. Boys.* They didn't know anything then. They were lost, and life was simple.

"Come on," Arnez said. He took his brother's arm. Mosquitoes buzzed in their ears—a desperate, starving moan.

Ted only said, "Wait," once, and then Arnez helped him into the passenger seat and closed the door.

Ted felt numb. The numbness crept up from his feet to his middle and eventually to his arms and into his lips. His cheeks ached, and he kept looking over at Arnez hoping he would see something in his face that would take away the numbness so he could cry, but there was nothing. Arnez stared at the road, his pupils still bulging from the alcohol. They drove and listened for sounds. The car stopped shaking, and the road was smooth and clear. A few cars passed them. Arnez sped up. He drank the rest of the whiskey. At the first opportunity, he turned around and headed back north. Neither looked when they passed the rest area. But when it was behind them, Ted turned around in his seat.

Arnez said, "It's practical. It's the thing you can afford."

"Maybe someone will find him," Ted said. "Find that cousin of his."

"Yeah," Arnez said, "maybe."

Ted said nothing. He had a little less than fifty dollars in his wallet, a little more than a thousand in his First National Bank account. He did some quick, rusty math. He could pay the bills this month, more than likely. The next month, the next, the next. They blew away from him like fallen leaves because none of it mattered now. Tomorrow didn't really matter, and how good that felt, Ted could not describe.

"We were supposed to go into Houston," Ted said.

"We're saving ourselves, Teddy," Arnez said. "That's all."

Once, years ago, their father had taken Ted on a trip across Missouri. They had ridden together and talked like people who often think about one another, who have something to say. It had been only them, the wind, and the sun, the bright shine off the car's hood, and the smells of cured hay. Late at night, they pulled into Kansas City. The lights hung over them, and Ted talked to his father about women and cars and drinking. As they drove through downtown, lost and looking for their hotel, Ted felt like a son.

But now, as they drove in the pale light of passing cars, he thought about that trip and how they hadn't connected at all. He'd tried. In a bar on the way back, his father had flirted with a waitress. She was buxom and loud and had a big smile and shiny red lipstick. She was everything common. His father, the man in the bathroom stall ten miles behind them, had squeezed her ass, touched her face. Ted had sat there wondering what it meant to be this man's son. Afraid he might not be able to go through with anything the old man had taught him: *Be yourself. Take care of each other. Here is better than anywhere else. Listen to your mother.* Neither brother had learned anything.

Ted stared out into the dark where he could begin to make out a town's soft glow shining above the road. He could see clouds of dust. Then, when they were closer, he could see the bugs hovering around the yellow streetlamps that lined the Interstate inside the city limits. He didn't know what town it was. He thought it might be Henderson, but then remembered they never made it that far. The map lay between them, with the road highlighted all the way to Houston. He crumpled it up, shoved it in the glove box, and tried to think of Marie Potts back in Wynott arranging flowers on caskets—her delicate, thin hands on the stems, sliding the blooms into place. His home seemed to exist in a different world. He could hear the echoes of his father's voice banging off the stainless steel walls.

"Boys," he called into the reflection inside the stall. "Boys?"

Ted saw the stall doors, the shine on them. He heard another sound, the sound of footsteps. "Boys?" came the call again, and he opened the door and found his father, smiling and shaking. "Thank God for you, Teddy," he said, and the echo bounced around the room, repeated itself. Then there was just the road, the lines in the highway white and yellow. Taillights lined up in front of them.

"You fell asleep," Arnez said. They were coming up on an exit with fast food restaurant signs blazing against the night sky. "Are you hungry?"

"Are you serious?" Ted asked. He sat up in his seat. "My God, Arnez. We've done something horrible." He put his hands on his head. "Turn the car around. Turn it around. We've got to go back."

"Like hell," Arnez said. "We're running for home now. We're done with it."

"Let me out," Ted said. "I want out."

Arnez's hand was faster than Ted's head. He caught Ted by the hair and pulled him toward his face, glancing away from the road.

"Listen to me," he said through his teeth, "that old shit is dead. Deader than you ever imagined him to be when you came up with this ramshackle idea. What do you think you were going to do? Find his long lost relative? Say, 'Hey there Cousin Whothefuck, want to take care of this dying old man?' Leave him sitting on the porch swing?"

"I don't know," Ted said. Tears came to his eyes. "I don't know. You're hurting me, Arn."

"Shit," Arnez said. He let go. "The old man's dead. That's all there is to it. He's dead."

"What if people ask questions?"

"What if they do? Say he came up to stay with me. He died while I was watching him, and we buried his old ass under that big Montana sky."

"What if they want a death certificate?"

"Hell, Teddy, I don't know. Get friendly with that Potts girl. She knows people down at the morgue. She'd probably do you a favor if you ask real nice."

"This is wrong."

"Yeah, well, there ain't much right about the world anyway."

Ted breathed in. He leaned back in the seat and thought of his father kicking at his seatback, his kicks like that of a child. Ted put his hand to his face. He huffed. He began to cry.

Another town faded behind them as the fast food restaurants and gas stations dropped away and left trees loaming just beyond the shoulder, flashing by in the headlights. They were only forty miles from Dallas. The road was good. It would take them home.

Play for Us

I t was an accident that Tom Liffkin had touched her. He'd come out of the arcade, his shorts wet from swimming in the water park's wave pool and cold now from being in the air conditioning, his College of the Ozarks Basketball Camp T-shirt limp on his shoulders and wet around the bottom. He glanced back at the game he'd just finished and could read his initials on the screen, even from where he stood. When he turned back, there she was, too close to dodge. He ran straight into her pillow-like chest. She reeled backward and shook her head. Her sleek body slipped past his pale one in two smooth sidesteps. She walked away on the balls of her feet, her ankles elevated in invisible heels.

On the painfully hot bus they rode back to the college campus, he didn't tell exactly how it happened. Everyone had seen the girl in the brown bikini. They had pointed her out as she slicked her arms and legs with tanning oil near the kiddie pool, as she lounged on a raft on the Lazy River, as she splashed water at the lifeguards. She was long and lean and, though no one said it, the one thing that really awed them was her age. Someone from camp found out she was only sixteen. Not older and unattainable; not younger and forbidden. It made her more and more of a goddess, someone to be sought and worshipped, and they did so, on the bus, quietly so as not to disturb the already sunburned and frustrated coaches who had reluctantly accompanied them on the one outing the camp promised. They spoke about her body, about her friends, who they all remembered as pasty—the color of dead people. They were teenage boys with imaginations and nothing else to do, and they were exceedingly hot on the bus.

They were there to play basketball under the summer's weighted heat, and one thing they dared not do was arouse any anger from the coaches at the front of the bus, their heads leaning forward on the seats, their arms folded in front of them. So they whispered. Tom Liffkin whispered. He told them all he had touched her, reached out for her. Touched first her arm and, as he told it, her neck, her breasts, her stomach. How she'd moaned. No one believed him. *Bullshit*, some of them said. But inwardly, they all imagined her in her brown bikini, with them, alone, in a bathroom at the water park, and how her bikini would shed. Some had her ripping it off, others removing it one piece at a time, and they thought about this the whole ride back, ignoring the go-kart tracks that had, on the drive over, fascinated them.

They thought about her while they sat beneath the oak trees that lined the small plot of grass in front of the gym. The heat rolled off their shoulders in streaks of sweat beads that gathered around their necks.

"I'd give it to her from behind," one said. "Wham, wham, wham." He put his hands out in front of him as if he were about to receive a football snap. Then a coach came out and barked at them to get off their asses, get in the gym. He herded them in at a trot, brought them in like a good sheep dog, and made them run ten wind sprints for wasting his time.

Tom Liffkin had a coach once who would shout at them before every game.

"Boys," he'd shout, "get your head out of your ass and play like a goddamn maniac tonight. Like a champion." He put his hands together as if he were praying. "These are the days that shape who you'll become, men. You've got to play your nuts off because you don't want to have any regrets. You don't want to run into someone thirty years from now and have them say, 'God, if you'd only tried a little harder.' Now do you, boys?"

"No," they'd answer.

"Play your asses off. You won't have another moment like this in your life."

After the games, Tom Liffkin would feel as if his legs were made of jelly, as if walking to the bus would be the last thing he would ever do because as he went up the stairs that led out of the locker room, his jelly legs would fail him. He would crumple down the stairs and land in a heap of misery, his legs searing with pain. There was nothing left for him to give at the end of a game. For a long time, that was perfect. He thought there was nothing better than to have left every ounce of himself on some basketball court somewhere in the middle of Missouri. There were bits and pieces of him scattered like cinder ashes blown across the landscape. He peppered the hills with his effort.

The boys slept on the floor of the second tier that ringed the gymnasium where the retractable bleachers were pushed back. They threw coins through the blackness. The coins bounced off walls and sleeping bags, making pinging noises on the gym floor. The coaches slept on cots in the room that housed the stairwell leading down to the main floor. The lights were kept on, and one coach made regular rounds to ensure the boys were still and asleep. Every thirty minutes, the on-duty coach would make the rounds. The boys had it timed so they feigned sleep as he passed.

Coach Markum was late for his round the evening after they returned from the water park. The boys lay cocooned in their sleeping bags, wrapped like gifts on the concrete floor. Tom Liffkin lay with them, his thoughts of the girl in the brown bikini, her soft skin. Coach Markum had decided to wait until his next scheduled round, and that's why he found Tom Liffkin in the corner with his pants around his ankles, his hand wrapped tightly around himself. Markum ordered him to stop as he stood over the crouching boy whose pants were around his ankles, whose hands were cupped around his crotch, concealing himself. Markum was backlit and dark, a shape more than anything else. There were snickers in the background. Tom Liffkin shuddered. He felt cold and tired. He shrank into himself in the corner as Coach Markum leaned down and took him by the arm, hauled him up, and began pulling him through the endless rows of sleeping bags where the boys lay feigning sleep. Tom Liffkin stumbled over his pants, and he heard someone laugh. Markum stopped and spun his head around.

"Get your asses to sleep," he shouted. He pulled Tom Liffkin up again, and they went on toward the lit stairwell door where the coaches slept. As the grip on his arm tightened, Tom Liffkin heard the boys talking behind him in low whispers that only the shamed can hear.

Tom Liffkin picked up a basketball at age eleven. By the time he was twelve, he still wasn't very good. By fourteen, he had become a slight disappointment to his family. He could shoot a little, and he could run. That was about it. In a game when he was twelve, he scored twenty-two points while the team only scored thirty-seven. His father took him to the Dairy Freeze after the game where he ordered them both chicken strip baskets and bragged to everyone within earshot of his son's basketball future.

"He'll play for Norm Stewart someday," his father said. Ranch dressing dripped from his lower lip as he spoke, laughed, and slapped Tom Liffkin's back until it was red. "He's got scholarship written all over him."

Tom Liffkin found himself engrossed with basketball. He found his parents attending every game. In the summer, he played in organized leagues. His father would yell at the pimpled-faced referee and once had to be dragged from the gym by a hefty principal. He was just good enough by the time he turned fifteen to garner some attention. The magazine that outlined each team from the Halverton Valley League mentioned his name toward the end of their article as a "player who could make a mark."

The high school season started. He fell in step with the others who took the sport seriously, trying to make ten out of ten free throws with their eyes closed, concentrating on learning a set of plays for the next game, going over scouting reports, and watching film of an upcoming opponent during study hall.

They sat in silence on the newest school bus as they angled down the weaving Ozark roads that split through where the hills dipped and then curved back in a switchback that pulled them toward the aisle or pressed them into the metal exterior. They played in isolated towns against teams they knew they could beat. The gym was always packed with old men who staggered up the bleachers, who had once played on the same floor they could now barely walk across. Young women shook their heads at them—*those* boys from *that* town—and whispered about their habits. Cheerleaders and students lined up to shout insults or to simply stare at people until the game started.

They played in tight little gyms that smelled of buttery popcorn, spilt Coca-Cola, and sweat under lights that turned the ball from orange to yellow. They were businessmen, entertainers of the highest caliber, a traveling show of agility and strength. Dressed to impress, their khaki pants, bought at Family Dollar, were threadbare at the waist and knees. They heard parents fight with one another. Occasionally the words turned into fists. They played hard because the faster they ran, the more the faces in the crowd would blur together to become nothing more than something else for them to run by. Tom Liffkin lived in all of this and didn't understand it. He only knew that when he was able to score, when he was able to make a difference on the basketball court, he mattered. At home, there would be smiles and hugs, but only if he did something. At school, people would notice him.

"For God's sake," his father told him once during his freshman year, "you've got to *do* something. I mean *something* out there. You look like a goddamn baboon picking its ass."

They reached the coach's room. The lights inside buzzed like a swarm of distant flies.

"Jesus, Phil. What are you doing?" one coach asked. He slipped a flask under his sleeping bag.

Tom Liffkin had never seen the coaches like this. They were raw and exposed in their underwear and pajama bottoms. Most of them looked like people he knew, like people who worked in gas stations and cleaned windshields for a living. He was scared, and his pants were still around his ankles.

"You want to know what this little shit did?" Markum asked. "I caught him over in the corner jerking off." The coaches looked down, and some of them began to laugh. "It ain't funny, goddamnit," Markum barked.

"Shit," one snorted, "he doesn't have any pants on."

Tom Liffkin reached down to cover himself.

"Let him go put some pants on, Phil," said the one who had hid the flask.

Coach Markum let him go. Tom Liffkin slipped out and ran past the sleeping bags. He ran until he was on the other side of the gym where he found a cubby between the bleachers and the wall. He burrowed in, hid, and cried.

The wind was cool and came through the open gymnasium doors the next morning. A whistle blew. The boys snapped to attention. They set their game faces and waited. Coach Markum walked up and down between them, his whistle bouncing off his chest. They were in lines in spaces assigned at the beginning of camp. They had to remember their space when the whistle blew. A few empty spots dotted the gym floor, boys who had gotten hurt and were leaning on crutches along the wall or had been sent home with concussions or broken bones. They were ready for anything because they never knew what kind of mood the coaches would be in, but they knew today that something was foul.

"I heard some kid got caught stroking his pecker," one whispered, and the whistle's blast rang out and burned their ears. Markum was up front now.

"There's some of you who ain't got their heads in the game," Markum said. He found Tom Liffkin standing in the second row of boys. He took his arm and led him up to the front. He ordered the rest of the boys to the push-up position, and they fell to the floor, prone, with their arms extended downward, holding up their own weight.

"There's some of you don't realize what you're doing here. You ain't got no pride in you. You think this is all some big game." He shook Tom Liffkin a little. "Going down some water ride and staring at tits all day ain't no way to make yourselves better. Look at where it gets you." He paused and looked at them. His eyes burned beneath dark, broad eyebrows. "There ain't a goddamn one of you ever gonna amount to anything." He was still shouting. "You're all shit.

Plain old shit. And some of you are bigger pieces than others," he said, staring down at Tom Liffkin whose skin felt as if it were pulling away from his body. "There ain't a damn thing worse," Markum said, "than a sorry ass pecker puller."

"Now," Markum said to Tom Liffkin, "make a circle with your fist." He demonstrated. "You measure 'em. Measure every damn one of 'em. And they better stay that far off the ground." He pointed at Tom Liffkin's fist and blew the whistle. "Go on," he said, "put that hand to some decent use. You sure as hell used it last night." The boys dropped down, and Tom began going around to each of them, placing his fist between their chins and the ground. The boys winced at the sight of his hand beneath their face.

"Jesus Christ," one said through heavy breath, "get that fucking thing away from me."

"Lower," Markum shouted, and Tom Liffkin kept on. The boys moaned. Pain rolled up through their legs and backs, which would ache for years because they were nothing more than horses. Their ankles stuffed with scar tissue, their backs in deep pain, their knees shot because of their blind devotion to people who, ultimately, cared little about them. They wanted to have no regrets.

Tom measured, and he regretted. He regretted the camp. He regretted the little ability he had to play the game. He thought about the girl in the brown bikini and knew why he was so lucky to have touched her.

It was an accident, but it was the purest thing he'd ever known. He placed his fist on the floor. The boy's chin came down.

Catching Earl

Once a week, on Wednesday, Ted goes to his group. It's a group about control—controlling anger, aggression, and rage—all in the basement of the First Methodist Church. It is run by a little, scrawny guy named Ernie who distributes weak orange soda. Orange soda. In the basement of the Methodist church. How can this be salvation, Ted often thinks. He looks at the soda can and at the other men listening to Ernie and feels a little silly sitting there. Then he thinks of Marie at home with her burn scars from sometime when he lost control and turns his soda can over and over in his hand and tries to stay focused.

Earl and Susan live in Ted's neighborhood, across the street. Ted can see their one-story ranch through the crabapple tree in his front yard. There is a small, tipped-over tricycle in the driveway. Ted believes Earl beats Susan. He believes this because of the way he has seen Susan act. She is guarded, always slumped over and as exhausted as a nurse after a double shift. And Earl? Earl is quiet enough, but there's something about him—perhaps it's his eyes or all the flannel he wears that makes Ted think Earl is up to something.

It is more about Susan though. When Ted looks at Susan, he sees Marie's younger self. It was when he realized Marie had lost her will that he fought the urge to fly off the handle, joined the group, and told her things would improve. She had lost her will to fight when their son, Danny, left for the Marines. He is fighting in a war now. Ted and Marie, their battles long fought, often sit in the living room, look at the pictures of him in his uniform, and cry at the thought of his possible death. Earl has a young daughter named Melissa, and they see her out on the front lawn every now and then, playing beneath the walnut trees and riding her tricycle alone down the middle of the street. Ted's perception of the situation across the street annoys him. He thinks if he says something it will, at the most, make him feel a little better, which is the only thing that matters to him anyway.

Wednesday night, Ernie challenges them with the old fall-into-your-partner's-arms game. They have played this one before, but Ernie says it is important to constantly reintroduce trust. Ted wonders how he will catch the monster he is paired with. The man weighs about 270, and none of it is muscle. Ted thinks about Earl and how he would fit in here. He looks much like the rest of them—small men, with small eyes and balding heads, except for the younger ones with slick hair or thin beards. Ted throws himself backwards into massive arms. His eyes are closed. He is so close to losing his trust in everything that he is nauseated. He feels the room spin. The black behind his eyes pulses, and Steak catches him. They call the heavy man Steak because that is what he likes to eat and talk about. He is always talking about the steak his wife used to fix him.

Ted wonders if Earl could accomplish any of this or if he is so far gone it is not worth it. But Ted can't get any of it out of his head—how Earl's wife and daughter cry when he comes home and how that sound can come across the street like a neighbor's leaves and through his windows, into his life with Marie while they contemplate the existence, dead or alive, of their son. Steak lets him go.

"Now me," he says and turns. Ted cannot see around him, and Steak is crossing his arms. Ted has a vision of letting him fall and the ruckus that would cause, but he is not sure he wants to piss off Steak. So he reaches out. The big guy falls back and Ted catches him. Then Ted falls backward, slipping. His wrists slam back as they hit the concrete floor and arch toward his forearms, jamming them. Pain ricochets through his arms. His wrists throb, but he pushes up. As Steak comes to a stand, Ted rolls on the floor, rubbing his wrists. Ted fumbles around, trying to get up. Steak offers him a hand, trying to preserve trust, but to no avail. When something bigger than you asks you to trust it, it is just a little too damn heavy.

On Saturday, Ted meets Earl on the sidewalk. They are both walking their dogs. Earl has his little schnauzer on a short leash. Ted walks his bull terrier. They exchange pleasantries and talk about fall approaching, how the leaves will cover their yards, and how those Chinese chestnuts from Dan Davies' yard will spill out all over the neighborhood, carried by wind and squirrels. They laugh at this.

Earl wears jeans and a red flannel shirt tucked in at the waist. He looks ready for hunting or a Lands' End catalog shoot. Ted is in his bathrobe because he feels comfortable in his neighborhood now; he feels as if he can walk around in his bathrobe. He has lived here for twenty-two years—he has earned the right. And besides, people don't look at him anymore anyway. They know about him, about how he used to be: the binge drinking, the job loss, and the beatings. Now he is different. Now he is a sad, old man in his bathrobe.

He likes the idea. It makes him feel as if he is one with the neighborhood. Earl is still young and can't walk around in a bathrobe. He has to be trimmed and proper. Earl tells Ted he is having a party this weekend to watch the football game.

He mentions something about moving forward, putting his life back together, and then says, "I'm only inviting a few people, but why don't you stop by. Just the guys. I'm buying the beer."

Ted thinks for a moment. Next Sunday. What is he doing next Sunday? Since he has been sober, he has trouble remembering his plans, but he knows it is only because he *has* plans. He can't think of anything and wonders what it will be like to see the inside of Earl's house. He is afraid it might be too familiar, but he decides he can take it when Earl presses. It is only a football game, after all. Even though he cares little for football, it is the local pro team, and that might be enough to catch his interest.

That Wednesday, Ernie asks about his son.

"Do you know where he is?" Ernie asks.

"No," Ted says.

"And how do you feel about that?"

This is one of Ernie's favorite things to do, make people sweat with questions that have no real answers—questions so complicated they give Ted a dull ache on the bridge of his nose. He answers this one the same way he answers all of them.

"I don't know," he says. Ted feels rage. It makes him hot underneath his clothes. It makes him feel as if he has never been able to really understand anything that goes on inside his own house, even after he quit drinking. How can his son walk off and never return? He doesn't know that he won't return, but he knows he will never see him again, just as sure as he knows that Ernie's questions will make his nose hurt.

"Work on that," Ernie tells him. Then to the rest of the group, "We've got to understand ourselves before we can begin to understand what limits us."

Ted is not stupid. He knows Ernie believes that he sobered up because Danny left and that it dug a hole in his life. Ernie believes each of them has lost something, like a son or a mother, and they need to reconnect with that loss on some level. These are the things he tells them at one-on-one meetings in the church office. He places his degrees from the University of Phoenix on the desk in frames leaned against stacks of books with titles like *Finding Your Inner Child* and *The Lost and Hopeful*. When he meets with Ted, Ted doesn't say much but does tell skinny Ernie how things are with Marie. Things are better, he tells him each time. Today we went on a picnic, a walk, or something to do with nature because Ernie likes to hear this. Whether or not he has actually done something like that really doesn't matter to Ted, but he knows things are better in some ways. He wonders what Earl would say in a meeting like that, if Earl would respond the same way.

Ted turns over his warming can of soda. Droplets gather around his fingers and make his hands clammy. Ernie is pairing them off. It is time to discuss the feelings they have had this week. Steak is paired with someone else, and Ted gets a little runt of a guy named Peter. He is only twenty-seven, but he looks much older. He has no hair, which makes him angry.

"I got so mad at Phil this week," he's saying. Peter is gay, and Phil fills him up. "I was so mad that I actually broke our Tiffany lamp. Can you imagine? I just broke it. Right there on the floor in front of him. He was so sad, and I love it when he is sad. It makes him look like one of those pound puppies, which makes me feel so good. Do you think that's why I broke the lamp? Because I like him like a pound puppy?"

"Yes," Ted says.

Peter leans back in his chair, crosses his ankles, and looks content.

"What about you? Did you commit any crimes this week?"

Ted says nothing.

Ted shows up at Earl's place. He is the last one to arrive. Dan Davies is there, sitting in the overstuffed easy chair; a guy who works at the gas station at the block's end is on the ottoman. There are only four people there, including Earl. When Earl comes in, he is wearing a sweatshirt that says "Rams" on the front. He offers Ted a beer. It is an import called Damm.

"Drink all the Damm beer you want," Earl says with a laugh. Ted takes the beer, settles in on the couch between Davies and the filling station guy. They turn on the game.

"We're playing San Francisco," Earl announces to no one. As he drinks, his moustache spreads over the top of the can, curling over.

"Are they good?" Ted asks. He feels a little out of place here among these younger men—men with vigor, men who don't need a hot shower each morning just to work out their joints. They all look at him at the same time, as if he is the kid in class with the stupid question. He sinks back into the couch again and wonders why in the hell he accepted the invite.

"They're all right," Davies says. Davies is closest to his age. He was at least alive in the sixties, and Ted thinks this gives them a bit of a connection.

When St. Louis scores, they all jump up and high-five each other. Ted tries, but he is late standing up. By the time he has risen, the other guys are seated. He doesn't understand the game. The strategy they keep talking about is beyond him. And though he knows how football is scored, it is difficult to keep track of each team's points. So he looks out the window and sees, across the street, his own house—

tiny and situated on the corner, hidden by the sprawling crabapple tree. The tree blooms once a year in spring. When it flowers, it smells like sweet apple spice. The blooms are light pink—the color of a baby's cheeks. It is the prettiest tree on the block, but it only lasts for two weeks. Then, as if it has lost interest or attention, the blossoms fade.

Behind it, he can see the house and thinks of Marie. She is baking a peach pie, and it will be done when he gets home. Baking takes up a lot of her time. He can see his windows. They are dark even in the daylight, and he can't see in. He wishes he could so he could have contact with something familiar. St. Louis scores again, and he is on top of it this time, up and high-fiving them all around. When he sits down, his back aches.

The game ends and Davies says, "That's a winner," and leaves without saying goodbye. No one seems to notice or care.

The filling station guy leaves, so it is down to two. Ted sits with Earl in the living room, watching the television. The couch is plaid and covered in a bright orange afghan that makes him itch. Ted reaches to scratch his back. As he does, Earl stands up and moves toward the door.

"Damn Chinese chestnuts," he says. The door is open. They can see the yard.

"Yeah," Ted says. "Say," he says, "how are things with you and Susan?"

The question feels ridiculous. What business is it of his? Susan hasn't been there the whole time. She took off for the grocery store before the game started. She had left before Ted made his way over, but he had watched her from his window, hidden behind the shade. She had a couple of plastic bags, her purse, and a book. Wherever she was, she was probably comfortable for now.

"Things are okay," Earl says. He comes back, sits next to Ted. "I guess."

"You know," Ted says, "I've heard you guys sometimes."

"Yeah?"

"Sure. It's pretty loud. I'm wondering what the other neighbors might think, if they might call the cops. What do you think?"

Ted isn't sure if Earl knows about his past. He wasn't around for it, but it may have made its way to him. Ted's past tends to follow him that way, through the tongues of others who had the experience.

Earl straightens up. "It's okay. We fight. A little. It's pretty stressful around here right now." He turns off the television and stares into the screen. "I mean, everything that's gone on." He straightens up, squares his shoulders. "I'm supposed to put things back together. That's what this weekend was about. Sort of."

Ted remembers a time when he saw Earl and Susan out on their front lawn screaming at one another—a real soap opera unfolding before their eyes. Melissa was there, crying. It was awful. "You should talk to someone," he says.

"We fight. I mean what do you expect?"

Ted isn't sure if this is directed at him.

"I mean with what's happened and all," Earl says.

"I meet with these folks, once a week, down at the church. We sit around and talk. That's all. We have a beer or two," Ted lies. "And we talk. That's all."

"What do you talk about?"

"You know. How to be in a relationship. How to be yourself. That kind of stuff. You have to understand yourself before you can understand your limits."

Earl gives him a funny half-smile.

"Why don't you come with me next week. It's not that bad."

The age gap between them hovers over Ted's head. How could this young kid who has a job in construction, who knows how to build things so they come out right, listen to an old, shaky man who wanders around the neighborhood in his bathrobe, who doesn't like to be noticed, who would rather sit in a soft chair and stare at the wall thinking about his son? How could those two people ever meet somewhere in the middle, or at First Methodist for that matter, and come up with the answers? But Ted thinks, here I am, sitting here on the young man's couch and really trying to reach out, trying to make things better for someone else. Maybe, Ted thinks, I'm getting better.

Earl says, "Can Susan and I both go?"

"It's for men only," Ted says. "I'll come by on Wednesday and see if you're ready. If not, you can wait. You have to go on your own terms." Ted finds himself echoing Ernie more and more, as if the man is taking up residence in the side pocket of his brain.

"That's fine," Earl says. "Thanks for coming. Good game, huh?"

Ted looks down at the television and says, "Yeah, good game. Around seven o'clock, then?" Then he confesses, "I don't care much for football." As he is walking home, Susan's car turns onto the street headed for home. As the car passes him, Melissa waves from the backseat. Susan has the window down and has the radio up very loud. Brown paper sacks are piled in the backseat around Melissa. He can see this as they drive by slowly, and he can hear the music—some rock from the seventies: "Jim Dandy," and he is glad he is not wearing his bathrobe.

He can't wait to get home and tell Marie about what he has done today, about the steps he has taken. There is a jump in his walk, something he hasn't felt for a long time. It makes him a little uneasy at first, but then he falls in line as the song comes back to him. *Jim Dandy to the rescue. Jim Dandy to the rescue. Go Jim Dandy. Go Jim Dandy.* Marie will be proud of him.

He shows up a little early that Wednesday, wearing his khaki slacks and navy blue sport coat and loafers. There are white specks on his shoulder, but he brushes them off. Earl is on his couch, and Susan is next to him. They are both looking at a blank television set, staring at the reflection staring back at them. Because they don't see him, Ted pauses before he knocks on the glass door. They look lonely there, with the cushions and a mound of silence between them. He notices Melissa is in front of them, cross-legged on the floor. She is also staring at the blank television. Family photos cover the top of the TV—Earl's family all together, closely knit. In some photos, there is a young boy; in others, he is absent. Ted knocks and disrupts the scene. Earl lets him in.

"You're early," Earl says.

"I'm sorry. It's just that I'm excited about this for some reason."

"It's all right," Earl says. "We're just finishing up here."

Ted smiles and nods at Susan and Melissa, who nod back. They are both lovely looking, each with dark, silk-brown hair and big eyes, so dark there is no visible pupil. This is a little haunting but at the same time enticing. It drags him right into their stares.

Earl speaks over his shoulder. "When I get back, we'll watch Jake's video, okay, the one with him walking across the living room?"

"All right," Susan says. "We haven't watched a video in a while."

Earl leaves the house. After a wave to the women, Ted goes, too. He wonders if Earl has told them where he is going and asks him as they climb into Ted's Volvo.

"No," he says. "I'm going to see how it all pans out. Then I might tell them. If it helps."

They drive to the church. The leaves are on the ground now, spread out under the trees, all brown. Mixed in are Chinese chestnuts, littered around the street with spindly, dry hulls. The church is not far. They say little on the way, outside of boring remarks about the weather.

At the church, Ernie has them gather in a circle, as he always does, and passes out the soda. One for each, he says, just like each week. Earl gives Ted a look of disappointment—the kind you give a bad waitress. Ernie begins by telling them about his week. He has had a few problems at home. The gutters are falling off his house, and he has a squirrel problem. The little shits keep eating his pecans. Some laugh as he tells the story, but Ted can see it bothers Ernie because he keeps looking down as he says these things. He is not really talking about the squirrels. They all know that because, in his weaker moments, when he is not feeling up to leading the group, Ernie breaks down about his wife, Linda, who died in a car crash. Ernie did time. Now that he is out, leading the group is part of his recovery. He shows them his tattoos sometimes. "Now," he says, "who would like to go first?" He goes around the circle with his eyes. Each man looks at the ground until he gets to a man named Raphael who looks right at him. "How about you, Raph?"

Raphael stands up. "So, I'm going to get the paper this morning, and this kid rides by on his bike, right? And this kid, he says 'Hey mister, get the fuck outta my way.' And I'm thinking, 'What the hell?' and this kid, right, he says, 'Get the fuck outta my way.' I took him off that bike and popped him in the nose, is what I did, see. Or what I woulda liked to done, see. I didn't do it cause it isn't right, but woulda liked to." Raphael sits down. Ernie gives him an approving smile. It is difficult to discern Ernie's thoughts. He has a way of smiling that takes over and doesn't let out what he really believes. Ted hates this. Earl is next.

"You're new to the group, yes?" Ernie says.

"Yeah."

"Why don't you introduce yourself to everyone."

He hesitates. "I'm Earl. Earl Dobson. I came with Ted."

The group, in unison, says, "Hi Earl."

"And why have you decided to join us?" Ernie asks.

"I guess to work on my marriage."

"Whose marriage?"

And the group says, in unison, "*Our* marriage."

Ernie says to Earl, "You need to recognize the cooperation between two people. That two people exist in your world and your actions hurt or help both of them."

Earl gives Ernie the same look Ted got when the soda was handed out.

"Four," Earl says.

Ernie looks at him, his face blank.

Earl says, "There are four people in my life."

"Good," Ernie says, "who's next?"

Steak is next. Steak stands up and gives a long-winded description of an argument he had with his girlfriend, Wanda, which escalated, but then was brought down to a discussion level. Ernie applauds when he finishes. They go around the circle. Ted had a few stories he cooked up when he started the group, and he rotates them weekly. It is not that he doesn't want something to tell, it is that he has nothing. When he told Marie about helping Earl, Marie took his hand, led him to the couch, and had him sit down. She pointed to the picture of Danny and said, "Look with me. Look at him." And they sat on the couch for the next hour just looking at the picture. Danny's uniform looked tight, wrapped on him like a cornhusk.

The time comes for the trust fall exercise. They partner up, and Ted is expecting Steak again, but he gets Earl. They stand on the far side of the room, away from everyone else.

"Look," Earl says, "this is a little embarrassing. What's this all about?"

"Control," Ted says.

"Control? Over what?"

"Over yourself." Ted wants to ask about him, his wife, and his daughter staring at the blank TV, but he doesn't.

"I have control," Earl says.

"I know," Ted says. "I know you do."

"Why do people think I'm out of control? My boss thinks I'm out of control, tells me to take a few days off. My sister thinks I'm out of control, tells me not to call her anymore. My father *is* out of control, and he thinks *I'm* out of control. What the hell?"

"We should do the exercise," Ted says.

"What is it?"

"You stand here," he says, pointing in front of him, "and fall back into my arms, and I'm supposed to catch you." Earl gives him the look again, only this time he cocks one eyebrow.

"That's it?"

"Yes."

"This is what you do?"

"Yes."

Earl shakes his head and takes his position in front of Ted. "I should go home," he says, "and be with my son. We're going to watch his video tonight. The one where he's walking across the living room. It was the first time." Earl moves in front of Ted. "I got the video the very first time he did that. How many people can say that?"

"Cross your arms," Ted says. "It makes it easier to catch you."

Earl does. He stands in front of Ted and crosses his arms. His shoulder blades sprout out of his shirt, little triangles. Ted can see around Earl, unlike Steak, so he can see the rest of the men falling into one another's arms and enjoying it, laughing and giggling like high school kids. It is a big game, he thinks, just one big game. He reaches down and rubs his jammed wrist. It still hurts a bit. Earl looks back at him.

"Now close your eyes," Ted says. Earl turns his head back. "Okay, whenever you are ready."

Earl falls, arching back and into Ted's arms where he lands against Ted's stomach. Ted reaches out and wraps his arms around Earl, feeling the man's weight sink against him, feeling the push against his spine as he digs in his heels. Earl begins to slip, falling, sliding out from under his fingers. Losing his balance, Ted stumbles back, slipping on the shiny linoleum floor. They tumble, both of them, to the ground.

The Same as Everywhere Else

A heat wave had its fingers wrapped tightly around us. People were dying in Paris. Everyone we met told us how many had died. But we weren't there. We were in Santiago, and we needed to get into the mountains.

"We could go to La Coruña," Harris said.

"No good," I said. "It's hot there, too. And the beaches are horrible."

"They've got girls," he said.

"If you want girls, we'll go to Barcelona, but I don't think we'll get out of the heat there either."

"Pamplona then. Up in the mountains. Or Bordeaux."

"I don't want to go to France," I said. "The French make me anxious." I was quoting our hotel matron. She had three Frenchmen who hadn't paid her yet and was upset about it. She threatened to throw them out, but they would just find somewhere else to pilfer, and, she said, she needed the promise of their money to make it through the day. It wasn't the real reason I didn't want to go to France. "There's nothing to do in Pamplona now," I said.

"Lisbon?" he asked.

"No," I said. "Too many people."

"San Sebastian then."

I stopped walking. We were near downtown Santiago where narrow streets twisted their way to the cathedral. Pilgrims came up the street burdened with packs, pushing themselves along with walking sticks. It was two days before the Feast of St. James, and already a crowd had staked itself outside the cathedral. The festivities would overwhelm everyone. In San Sebastian with the Basques, things would be quieter.

I pulled my pack of cigars out of my shirt pocket. They were the little kind you could find anywhere in the States, but here it was more difficult. I wondered if I could find them in San Sebastian. I knew I could get them in France. I had found these in Bordeaux, but I didn't want to go up there just for cigars. I wasn't going to France at all. I had half a pack left, and I shook one out and offered another to Harris. He took it, and we went on.

"Good," I said. "Let's get the tickets."

We went to tell our matron we were leaving. After we paid her, she took us down to the bar and bought a beer for each of us.

"For your trouble," she said.

We drank and sat around a while, watching the pilgrims walk by. They didn't look like pilgrims. They looked like tourists with good intentions. More people gathered at sidewalk tables. Together, the group was big but not loud. Harris and I talked about what I had been studying in Madrid before I left. I told him about Laura again, a story he had already heard. One of the things I could tolerate about Harris, especially then, was his ability to listen and not hear. One of the members of the big group leaned over toward us.

"American?" he asked. He was a broad German. The town was full of Germans.

"Yes," I said.

"I hate Americans," he said.

"Me, too," I said.

He laughed and raised his drink. "You're here for the festival?"

"No," I said. "We're leaving for the festival."

"We're not here for the festival either," he said. His blonde hair glowed in the early sun. "We're going to Portugal for a football match. Do you like football?"

"I've grown accustomed to it," I said. Harris nodded.

"Most Americans don't," he said. He raised his hand, waved it a little from side to side. "Some do."

"Why did you stop here?" I asked.

"To see this place. We've heard of this place."

"It's a good town," Harris said, a little too loud. People looked at him. "Nice people."

"You should come with us," the German said. "I like you."

"We're going to San Sebastian," I said. "To get out of the heat."

"Nothing but trouble there," he said. "We come from there. They are blowing up buses again."

"We like to walk," I said.

"You will do plenty of it."

"You should see a bullfight," Harris said.

"I have seen them," the German replied. "Nothing much to it. Bullfights are for Spain. Not for Germany." He took another drink. He said, "But football. That is for everyone."

He turned away. Harris and I finished our drinks. We paid our matron, who thanked us and blessed our journey. Then she went back upstairs saying she would throw the French out because we had paid her. It felt good to give someone more than just a promise.

We went down to the station and bought our way out of the heat: two tickets to San Sebastian by way of Vitoria. Harris had a friend there who taught at the American English

Institute. He wanted to say hello. I had no objections. I had no job to speak of, just living on the skim of what I had earned right after college, living on the edge of nothing. We had underpaid for our room, but we had overpaid for other things—all in the same moment. That was the thing about Spain: You could do nothing and something at the same time.

The train came late, which put us back an hour. Harris called and let his friend know we would be late, and the friend found that acceptable—part of the culture, he said. It kept him from canceling a class, which made us feel better. We stood on the platform and watched the incoming trains unload. People swarmed off and headed for the town or the bar, depending on which desire hit them first. The platform was crowded with backpacks, luggage, and people leaning on concrete pillars. Some slept on the benches. It was still hot underneath the canopy.

"Damn heat," I said. "Can't get away from it."

"You can run," Harris said, but he didn't finish his thought because I gave him my don't-you-dare stare.

The pigeons around our feet all stood on one foot; they panted and searched for scraps.

"We're trying," Harris said. We stood still for a while, watching the people. Then Harris said, "I heard Laura's going back to the States." It was as if he had been waiting to say it, waiting for the tension to hit the right peak, as if he had actually heard things all along and had stored them for this moment on the platform. Our soles were burning.

Laura was part of the reason I was in Santiago in the first place. I hadn't even withdrawn from my graduate classes. The night Laura told me she was leaving, I caught a train at the Atocha Station and met Harris in Seville. We went north from there to Santiago with a stop in Porto where we frequented the port houses. I don't know what I was looking for. I thought I might find some comfort, but the liquor hadn't brought any, religion either. Now we were headed for the mountains, running from the heat. I thought it all a little pointless.

"No," I said. "She's not going back."

"Where is she going?"

"Paris," I said.

"Hell," he said, "that's not far. A day by train."

"It's far enough," I said.

"You're acting stupid."

"Let's just get on the train," I said. Ours was coming in. The train doors opened, and the people swarmed the platform like agitated bees. I thought I could feel the platform moving underneath me, all those people weighed down with their belongings strapped to them; they looked like oxen pulling carts. They moved like cattle, a slow stream through the station doors, up the hill, prodding along toward a cathedral where they would adore something they had been told was the truth.

We made our way through them—swimming against the current—and finally onto the train. It was nearly empty, and we found our seats without a problem. No one was in them. The horn sounded, the pressure brakes let loose, and we began rolling out. It felt good to have Santiago behind me.

We sat opposite one another, played cards, and drank stale Spanish beer. The train rocked east and south, passing through little towns with five-minute stops. A bigger town earned a twenty-minute stop, so we had a sandwich in the station bar. It took almost three hours to reach Vitoria.

At the station, we found Harris's friend waiting outside.

"This is Cayle," Harris said to me. "Cayle, this is my friend from the University. I told you about him."

"Yeah," Cayle said. "Good to meet you." He had a balding head and thin shoulders that came square and made him boxy. Smart-looking glasses rounded his eyes with thin rims that barely showed. The temples disappeared into his thin hair. He had a good look.

"Same," I said.

He reached over and slapped Harris on the back. "Stick with this guy and you'll be staring up at your toes before morning." They both laughed. Cayle said they were frat brothers. Knitted together by nothing, I thought as they shook hands.

We went out to Cayle's Fiat and drove through streets that met at right angles and past modern buildings to his apartment near the center of Vitoria. I thought I had wound up back in the States.

"This town," Cayle said, shifting the Fiat frantically, "is not like anywhere else. I've never seen so many serious people."

"What about you?" Harris asked.

"I'm as serious as they come," he said. There was something about him that I understood. He reminded me of a former roommate who used to talk big about things he didn't know or understand. I always liked him because he made me look smart. I thought we would have a fine time—the three of us.

We settled in at the little two-bedroom apartment. Our train for San Sebastian didn't leave until mid-morning the next day.

"What do you want to do?" Cayle asked. "I could call some girls."

"Call them up," Harris said. "We've been thinking about girls for a while. The ones in Santiago are all so cloistered. It's like they are tied right up around St. James's neck." Harris turned to me. "Besides," he said, "Timmy here needs a girl. His left."

I glared at him.

"Been there," Cayle said, and he called the girls who said they would be over in a few hours. While we waited, Cayle poured us drinks. A couple drinks later, the river of conversation was undammed.

"How are things here?" Harris asked.

"Shitty," Cayle said. "These people don't know what they want. They protest outside the Institute. Some of them want us to stay. Others want us to leave, but they all want in the door. It's crazy."

"That's fanaticism," I said.

"No," Cayle said. "Fanatics at least know what they want. These people are just confused."

"We ran into some Germans who said there is no confusion in San Sebastian."

"Is that why you're going there?" he asked.

"Partly," I said, though it was much more than that. I had been confused since I left Madrid, and I wanted some stability, a place that left me thinking a specific way with no holes in the theories.

"There is never any confusion in San Sebastian. Except in the portrayal of it."

I was confused. I looked it.

"It is beautiful and horrible in the same instant," he said to me. He should know. He lived and worked in the Basque capital.

"Isn't that the way with Spain," Harris said.

"It's the way with most places," Cayle said.

We had another round of whiskey that tasted good. It was lighter than the beer and not stale and harsh on my stomach. We waited for the girls, and I felt a little light around the middle, as if my top parts were separating from my bottom parts. Vitoria wasn't so bad. Not so bad. It had a feel to it like something could happen there. Someone might say something that made perfect sense for the whole world, but no one would hear it coming out of a capital of a country that didn't exist.

There were four girls, putting the odds in everyone's favor. We decided to go out to a bar. I landed with a girl who told me to call her Kiki. She had brown, short hair that hung down to her eyes, which were green dots in her head. Her dark complexion waved in the night air—warm and muggy. The grip of heat was still on us. We laughed in the bar, and she tried to teach me the Basque words for *bathroom* and *beer*.

"If you are going to San Sebastian," Kiki said. "you will need to know things."

"I know things," I said, my head light now.

"You know nothing," she said. "Where are you from?"

"America," I said.

"Yes," she said, "you know nothing. Why are you in Spain?"

"I'm studying in Madrid."

"Nothing to learn in Madrid," she said.

"I've learned a few things," I said.

"You've learned nothing," she said. "What do you expect? Enlightenment?"

I said I didn't know what to expect.

"Then you are lost," she said. "There's no hope for you."

"Religious zealous," I said.

She laughed. "You're funny," she said. Then she got serious again. "I think you expect to find something, but there is nothing to find. This is the same as everywhere else. You Americans. That is what you do. You search for yourselves, yes?"

"You read too much," I said, trying to be funny.

People wearing professional clothes walked by the window. We sat around a table in the low light streaming in from the street.

"You got a girl?" Kiki asked.

"Yes," I said.

"What's her name?"

"Kiki," I said.

"Don't be stupid," she said. "What's her name?"

"Laura," I told her.

"In Madrid?"

"Yes," I lied, thinking of Laura. She would not come up to Kiki's shoulders. Her small frame nearly invisible.

"Why did you leave?"

"To visit him," I said, pointing at Harris.

"Stupid reason," Kiki laughed. "You love her?"

"Yes," I said. "What about you? You have someone?"

"A husband," Kiki said.

"Where is he?"

"He is in Paris," she said. "Roasting right now."

"What does he do?"

"He is *European*," she said, scrunching her face. "That is what he does. He travels around being *European*." She paused, looking down into her lap. Then she said, "Isn't that what it is all about? A man from Madrid travels to Paris. A man from Paris travels to Frankfurt. A woman from Frankfurt travels to Rome."

I nodded.

"Tell me," she said, "how many times have you moved in your life?"

I thought about it. I counted on my fingers. "Ten," I said.

"Including this one?"

"This isn't a move," I said. "It's a visit."

"We will see," she said. "That is what it is all about now. Moving. Relocating." She looked at me and at my clothes, up and down. She pulled out a cigarette, lit it, and drew in the smoke. As she blew it out, she said, "It is all very American, yes? A new life in a new place."

"Maybe it's for the best," I said.

She touched my face. Her touch felt as soft as angel wings, the kind you hear about in songs. She leaned over and kissed me, brushed her lips against mine, against my cheek. She smelled salty sweet. I kissed her back.

We all returned to Cayle's apartment. Two girls went with him. Harris left with one, and Kiki and I fooled around on the sofa. The night spun around us in perfect rows of streets laid out in blocks, in old cathedrals dressed up modernly, and in punctual squares, always around when you needed a bench and a flock of pigeons to feed. *Vitoria*, I thought, fading to sleep with Kiki under my arm, *capital of the world*.

In the morning, the girls were gone. Cayle fixed an American breakfast of eggs and toast. We sat around the small table in his apartment.

"I hope there are girls like that in San Sebastian," Harris said.

"You'll be fine," Cayle said. "What time do you leave?"

"Ten-thirty," I said.

"Smart of you to get a late train. Nothing gets going until at least eight." He stood up and drank more coffee. "I have a class," he said. He went out the door. "Just be sure to turn the lock when you leave."

He left us, and we knew we would need a taxi to reach the station on time. Harris said if we left then, we could walk it, but my head kept bobbing up and down. I never have held my liquor well, and the whiskey got me. The whiskey and Kiki.

I decided to shower. There was a little window in the bathroom, providing a view of the street. We were up higher than I realized, and I could kind of see the city and how it moved around with quickness so unlike anywhere else I had been in Spain. There was an authority, a get-things-done feel. The people moved with purpose, not the kind in Santiago where they moved in religious step. Here they had the proof that what they were doing made sense.

I got out of the shower and let the steam build up on the windows for a while, just to block it all out, especially the light. Then I went to the kitchen where Harris had things clean and looking nice.

"You going to shower?" I asked.

"Yeah," he said. When he entered the bathroom, I went out on the little balcony to smoke. I only had a few cigars left. I lit one and let the end flame a little before I puffed and blew the smoke out into the early heat. Already the concrete burned under my sock-covered feet. I could see the birds shaking themselves and dipping back into a puddle that had formed at the corner where a shopkeeper had sprayed the sidewalk. The puddle would be gone before noon, and the birds were anxious. From the balcony, I saw we were three stories up, that the city squatted, with a few exceptions. I thought maybe that was why no one noticed it, because it sat so low on the horizon. A city north of Madrid but nothing you could see from there. No skyscrapers to intimidate, no long boulevards to impress. It made me a little sad.

Harris joined me and was rubbing a towel on his black hair.

"Kind of a depressing, shitty town," he said.

He was right. It meant nothing. We had to leave. Soon he would call a taxi, or I would. We would be on a train to a different place that would have the same thing to say. He asked me for a cigar, and I gave him one, which left me with two. I stuffed them in my pocket and packed my bag. We went down to the street where we found a cab.

On the train, the town pulled away from us. I didn't think about it. I watched as we rolled past the blank houses and apartment complexes. All of them the same, with little balconies where people were smoking. I didn't think about it. I sat back in my seat and watched Harris play Solitaire and waited until all I could see were fields and looming mountains. I wanted to get up in those mountains for a breath of fresh air.

The Feast of St. James was one day away. We could tell by the number of people flooding the streets. It was difficult, but we managed and found a room at a little place on a back street—one the tourists didn't, couldn't, or wouldn't hit. It had high ceilings and walls painted a dull and chipping yellow. Lazy fans spun above us; you could see the gathered dust drifting like moss from the blades. Only a few people were staying there, and we had our own key to the front door. The patron was an old man with curly gray hair and a thick beard. He sat in the office all day watching the matches in black and white and getting upset at the referees and players. He cursed at them in Basque (I'd learned some of the words from Kiki, on the sofa), but he spoke Spanish to us, which made it easier.

"They don't know anything," he said when we paid him. "The bastards don't know anything. All the calls are wrong."

On the second floor, our room had a little balcony, but you had to climb out a window to reach it. Someone had welded iron flower boxes to the balconies, but there were no flowers in them, and the sun baked the iron to a deep black. Even here it was hot, but not like it was in Vitoria, not like in Santiago, and certainly not like Paris or Madrid where sheer numbers and concrete raised the temperature by at least ten degrees.

We sat in the room a while, listening to the sounds coming

through the thin walls. A radio. The ocean. Seagulls. A moan now and then. So very quiet and busy. I thought about Laura moving around in Paris. She would fit in well there with her high heels, short skirts, and small body. The French would like her. She had their mannerisms. I always thought that way, even though I loved France, enjoyed the wine, the food, even the people. Then I thought about jumping on a train and going to find her to try to convince her to come back. I imagined us meeting at a little café, eating a lunch of garlic potatoes, and talking about our life together in Paris. I would take her to the Musee D'Orsay because she loved the Impressionists, and we would walk along the Seine in the evening, feeding the pigeons little scraps of hard French bread. All Paris ever was to me was a mirror of some perfection.

Harris sat in his bed, leaning against the wall.

"Got anymore of those cigarettes?" he asked.

"They're cigars," I said, thinking of the two I had left, "and no, I don't have any."

"Damn," he said. "I could go for a smoke."

"You usually do," I said. I felt tired, the tired you feel after traveling through a country that never seemed to move under you. I was irritable.

"Don't be that way," he said. "You just need to get out a little. Isn't that what this trip is about?"

"I don't know," I said.

"When you called," he said, "you said you needed to get away. Well how much further away do you want to get?" He spread his arms, palms up. "This is the end of fucking everywhere."

I looked around the room. The cracked plaster walls. The useless ceiling fan. The dirty floor. Sheets with brown stains on them. The dry sink with a single spout. Out the window, I could see the date trees waving. San Sebastian blew right in—the smell of blood, the ocean salt, the trees, and the hot cobblestone streets.

"I could go for a drink," I said.

"Now, that is the spirit," Harris said. He put on his shirt. "We'll eat, drink, find a girl or two, and come back here."

"I don't want to find girls," I said. "I've been hunting girls all my life. I'm through with it."

"You've lost it," he said.

"It's stupid," I said. "And boring."

"You're a mess."

He went out, and I sat for a while on the end of my bed, near the window. I watched the sun lower over the city and the buildings light up like sparks from a fire. My head hurt, and I didn't feel like doing much of anything other than sitting on the bed watching the lights. When I stood, my head swam and caused me to lean on the wall. The paint cracked under my palm and left dusty yellow flakes all over my hand. I wiped it off, splashed some water on my face from the leaking faucet, and told myself things were okay. I told myself that I didn't miss her, that I hadn't made any mistakes in my life, and that San Sebastian provided me with a new chance to outrun the heat. Downstairs, I found Harris waiting by the desk. The football match was still on. Both of them were sweating; the old man's armpits were bluer than the rest of his shirt. They were talking about something. I couldn't pick it up, or I didn't want to. I shut that valve off. I wasn't listening anymore.

Wind blew in off the ocean and smelled of fish. We strolled along the streets, bought prawns from a vendor, and ate them raw. They were sweet and tender. We tried to read the signs written in Basque. We found graffiti in English. *Welcome tourists*, it read. *You are no longer in Spain. You are in the Basque Country. Welcome.* Beneath it was more. *Pick up a gun and kill a Marine for fun.*

We went into a tapas bar and ate shrimp, mussels, and crabmeat fried in garlic butter. We drank beer and felt settled.

"This is great," Harris said. "Want to get some dinner?"

"No," I said. "Let's find a place to really drink."

"Let's find some girls," Harris said. "Let's go to the beach."

"There aren't any girls here," I said. "I haven't seen any."

"They're here," he said. "They are just hiding."

"Why would they hide?"

"The same reason anyone hides. They don't know better."

He had been drinking. He downed his beer in a single drink.

"You're moving a little too fast," I said.

"Hell with it," he said. "I'm going to the beach. Meet me there if you want."

He left. I sat in the tapas bar with people around me speaking a language I didn't know, didn't care to know. It was the eve of the Feast of St. James. People were anxious and reserved. Tomorrow they would erupt in an explosion of celebration and restraint until nightfall. Then they would let it loose—whoop it up, as we say back home. But now they were slow about themselves. I went out into the street and down to another road, all with names I couldn't pronounce, with words that used the letter X as a vowel. I found a little place that sold pizza and went inside.

I was alone in the place. Other people sat at tables outside, but there were no outdoor tables available. So I sat at the bar and waited for someone to ask me something I understood. Behind the bar, a man was making pizzas. He slid them into the oven and quickly turned to start another. At the same time, another pizza came out the oven's other side. He saw me, but he didn't do anything. A waitress walked behind me. Her elbow brushed against my back. The man behind the counter kept working. Another person came in, sat down at the bar, and began playing a slot machine that hung on the wall. I waited. The man kept working. He had fast hands, flashing along with the knife he used to slice the dough. The pizzas flew by. He stopped suddenly, looked at me, and picked up a butcher knife that he had stuck in a carving board. He ran the blade up and down a sharpening rod, grinding the slick metal thin. He had a thick mustache and thin eyes and ears that punched out of his wrangled black hair.

I called out to him in Spanish, and he came over.

"The bar is closed," he said. "Eat outside."

"I'm not hungry," I said.

"Then leave," he said.

"I've heard this town is different," I said to him. He leaned down over the bar, and I could smell his breath coming through his beard. "I've heard it's a good place to make a start."

"It's different," he said. "Much different than anything you've ever seen."

"I'd like to see," I said.

"No," he said. "You should go." He raised the knife and pointed it at me. Its tip hovered just in front of my nose. I wasn't afraid of it here with the sunlight coming through the open door and the pizzas sizzling and steaming behind him. Then he switched on me, barked something in Basque. I stood up, a little shocked. He said, "See, this is not the place for you."

Sticking up from the counter stood a Budweiser beer tap. Bright red, like a flag.

I left and went to find Harris.

I stopped in a couple of clubs on the street that ran along the beach and didn't find him there. I began asking people if they had seen a loud American maybe with some girls. Most of them laughed at me, young people with arms slung around each other. One girl threw up her arms and shrugged.

I saw him then. Houses up in the hills around the bay made points of light lower than the horizon and above them were the stars. Behind me San Sebastian burned streetlamp yellow. On the beach, I saw Harris walking in the wet sand alone. His bare feet left shallow footprints. I started to call out to him. But then I saw ahead of him, about fifty feet, walked a woman wearing a dress that blew in the cool ocean wind. You could see the end of the beach where the pier jutted out and made the waves break sooner than anywhere else, but you could only see the lights. Harris kept following her. The waves came up close to his ankles as the tide barreled in. The woman stopped and looked out in the bay where people stood around on anchored boats draped with Christmas lights. There was nothing but the sound of waves and the murmur behind me. Harris caught up to her a little. When she saw him, she took off again, faster now. He quickened his own pace, and together they jogged off toward the pier. Soon the black beach swallowed them, and all I could see were the pier lights, the stars, and the boats bobbing up and down.

I went back to the room. I stood on the balcony, lit a cigar, let the wind take the smoke away, and felt sweat beads on my upper lip. The room was small: two beds, a little TV that only brought in two channels, a fan, a little table where our personals were piled up, and a hard tile floor that chilled my feet even during the hottest times of day. I tried to think of where Harris would go, but I only had inclinations. I didn't know the town. I didn't even know where I was. I thought about the game my family used to play at Christmas. We tried to decide if we went into Walmart where we would look first for each person in the room. I always ended up in the travel section, looking at travel books and luggage, always running away, even in Walmart. *Forlornly*, was the word they had used. *We would find Timothy looking forlornly at some expensive backpack.*

I could hear firecrackers exploding somewhere. I turned off the light and went downstairs where I found the old man watching another match on television. He leaned forward, his bright brown eyes on the screen.

I asked if I could watch with him. He drew up another chair and gestured toward it. He offered me a drink, and I took it. It was a sweet mixture, something with Coke in it, liquor too, rum maybe.

We watched the match between Real Madrid and Lisbon. The game went back and forth, and the players kept moving all the time. Soccer players amazed me, how they ran without ever seeming to tire. I felt worn, as if my whole body had been snatched and tumbled by a riptide. The old man scoffed at the players.

"They are pawns," he said to me. "They do not know what they are doing. They listen to the referees and the coaches. They ruin the game." He drank then—a long drink that seemed to bring him down a little. He settled back in his chair so our elbows nearly touched. "It is not the same," he said. "Nothing is the same as it used to be. It is all flawed."

He had the ceiling fan on, and I could feel the breeze. I could see the dirt on the floor lifting and falling, the clumps of cat hair bouncing around like tumbleweeds. He refilled my drink. For a while, I didn't think about Harris, the heat, Santiago, my family back home, or Laura in Paris. All I thought about was how the match was rigged; how the whole thing was flawed; how all they did was follow, follow, follow; and how I couldn't stop it. For a moment, I wanted to be more like Harris, who could shoot from one thing to the next without stopping to think about it. One girl to the next. One drink to the next. Nothing in between except the seams that he jumped over as if they were cracks in the sidewalk. Outside I could still hear the fireworks, soft pops in the night. People passed by the window. Some of them were obviously drunk. None of them were Harris. I knew he was gone.

I shook my last cigar out of the crumpled pack and handed it to the old man who took it and lit it. The fan blew the smoke around. I could see him through the smoke, his eyes still on the television, his hair up around his ears, his fingers on the cigar, watching the match and making perfect sense.

I Just Found This Hat

The end of the world will be something to see. That is what I tell my father when I take him for breakfast at the IHOP on Sundays. This is part of our routine, something he can handle, something he may need. While we are there, I fill his head with silly thoughts about the end of the world, how I'll watch from the living room television.

Today at IHOP, he tells me to shut up. He tells me flat out, "Shut up. You sound stupid." My mother has been dead for seven years, and he has these moments when he sounds just like her, as if she is popping right out of his mouth. The flies buzz on the window, the waitress shouts an order, and a bell rings. The smell of coffee, grease, and toast fill the room. My father sits hunched over, looks at me, and says, "Shut up" again. He repeats it over and over, and I slap his face.

I'm frozen. Around us, people keep eating. I listen to the soft clink of silverware on plates. Dad is quiet. He looks down into his lap like a child. I can feel the heat crawling over my cheeks. I stare out to the parking lot, thinking of how I can get out there without taking Dad with me, leave the evidence sitting in the booth with a red mark smearing one side of his face. The IHOP moves along as if nothing has happened. People are huddled over their pancakes, sausage, omelets, and stacks of butter-saturated toast. Over my shoulder, I hear the waitress asking the people behind me where they are from because she noticed their car: the license plate is different.

"We're from Idaho," the lady says. "We're on our way to New Orleans."

I find their car. Dust cakes the sides. Someone has rubbed *Wash Me?* into the dirt. The couple is old, like Dad, and they are going to New Orleans. The heated seat makes my legs ache, and I think about how nice it must feel in Idaho in summer, how walking outside must be like dipping a foot into a spring-fed river, how the mountains must blaze bright purple in the sun. How nice it would be to step into something like that for just a moment, to feel as if I am truly free. I am dreaming all of this when the waitress reaches our table.

"Everything all right here?" she asks. She holds a tray in the crook of her arm. She is slender all over. Her dress fits tightly around her waist where it is cinched with a yellow sash. Dad reaches out and touches her arm. She pulls back a little, just far enough to get away but doesn't say anything.

"We're fine," I say to Dad's face. He is looking at the waitress, but he is not really looking at her as much as he is staring at her yellow sash. He reaches for it.

"Don't touch that," I say, and he sinks into his side of the booth, sliding away from the waitress. He turns his head toward the window, and I can see the long red mark my hand left. I think about how I used to ride around on his back like a horse and how he used to hold me up close to the ceiling so I could see the tiny cracks in the plaster. The waitress leaves the check. She signs it: *Thanks, Have a good day Jenny.*

◆ ◆ ◆

My relationship with my father is friendly when his Alzheimer's doesn't fuzz his memory. I am the son he bonded with some time ago, or so I think and he let me believe. My older brother, Arnez, lives on a ranch in Wyoming, so he rarely makes it back to Missouri. I call him once or twice a year, around the holidays, and give him the whole scoop on Dad. He grunts into the phone and asks things like, "What kind of pills do they have him popping now?" And I tell him how Dad gets up each morning and has to take a shower, a four-hour marathon in the bathroom because he has trouble remembering the location of his hair gel, the dryer, his deodorant, and his aftershave. My father always primped himself slick and shiny like the chrome vacuum cleaners he once sold. Now I stand near the bathroom door because he might accidentally stick his finger in the outlet. Lately, I tell Arnez I have been walking away from the door, leaving him to his own fate. He won't remember it in twenty minutes anyway. I say time is squeezing in on him like a pressed lemon, which is what I'm usually doing when I'm talking to Arnez. It reduces the stress.

The day after I hit Dad, I sit alone on a park bench and watch the people pass by. A man wearing a big, ten-gallon cowboy hat approaches me, walking bowlegged. He tips his hat and says, "Howdy. How's things?" If I were a gay man, I think I would like this, but I'm not. I've been labeled though, but I'm not.

"Things are good," I say. I'm looking mostly at the hat. It blocks out the sun, and it's white, blazing. The sky around it makes it seem to hover just above his head. It's big enough to shadow his facial features. It's not comical, just big.

"You know," he says, "I'm not really a cowboy. I just found this hat."

I wonder why he is talking to me, but maybe he is just being friendly. This town isn't big. Big enough not to know everyone, but not big enough to feel overwhelmed in. It is the type of town you would forget you were from if you ever "made it" in life, got rich, starred in movies. It is the kind of place people joke about, the kind of town where people greet you whether they know you or not.

"You play the part well," I tell him. He gives me a nod and spits on the sidewalk. His spit is white and bubbly there at my feet, and he spreads it out with the heel of his black leather boot.

"I wear this hat so nobody will fuck with me," he says. "It makes people stand back and think I'm crazy."

I want to say, *Maybe you are*, but I don't. People walk around the bench. Cars pass. To our right, a lady lets her dog pee on a fire hydrant. Across the street, a man bends over a fruit stand and examines the peaches. It is warm with a gentle breeze. Everywhere—except where I sit—appears normal.

"Look," he says, "I've seen you in the IHOP. You eat pancakes and bacon with two eggs over easy every Sunday. I've seen you here, too. You're here about every week. Right here on this bench like you're trying to catch up to yourself or something. I've seen you at the IHOP with that old man who orders grits and sausage, a bagel, and green beans. Damn, that's a weird order. What's his diagnosis?"

I wait because now I know this fake cowboy. I've seen his face behind the counter, working over the grill, flipping the pancakes with a swift twist of his wrist, rolling the sausage links around, and toasting the melt sandwiches. I remember him without the hat. He seemed smaller every other time I'd seen him. Insignificant in his white apron and paper IHOP cap; his hair stuffed into a hairnet.

"Look," he says, "we've all been there before where you can't hardly stand to look at yourself." He sits down on the bench, which bows slightly away from me. "I've seen it hundreds of times. I used to work as a maintenance man at the nursing home. So, does he live with you?"

I say, "He's my father."

"Where is your mama?"

"She's dead," I say.

"It's a shame. Too bad. I've put two parents in the ground myself. I can't say it's an easy thing to go through. Although my mother was a helluva lot easier than my pap. He was one wildcat. We had to lock the lid to keep him in." He laughs a little. "Here," he says holding out his hand, "let's shake hands like normal people. That's what normal people do." I shake his hand. "I know it's tough, but there are people who want to know about this kind of thing. Lawyers and stuff. People who'd like to get their hands on a little money, or you, or whatever. The house, shit like that. If you have one. Hitting old people is the kind of thing people like to know about. I'm not up to telling them," he says. "Not if you can help me reason why I shouldn't."

"What do you want?" I ask.

"A little cash. That's all. Ten, twelve grand."

"I sell used cars," I say. "I don't have that kind of money."

"Sell more cars," he says. "You've got time. I'm in no rush." He is standing now—tall, lean, and frightening underneath his hat. "See you on Sunday," he says and tips his hat as he bowlegs down the sidewalk. He is clownish from behind, and he sidesteps a group of pigeons who feed on stale bread scattered around a dumpster.

When I get home, Lotta, the woman who watches Dad while I'm out, is sleeping on the couch. My father is nowhere to be seen, and I shake Lotta. She wakes up slowly, as if movement hurts.

"Where is he at?" I ask. "Where?"

"Calm down, now," she says. "He is upstairs, locked in his room. He wanted to be in there. I knew I was about ready to fall down, so I locked him in."

There are shadows in the room's corners. They peek around the end tables. They stretch like mice out of cracks. They are long and low.

"You should tell me when you're going to be longer than three hours. I can't keep up with him. I'm not so young myself."

I sit next to her. The couch is old and sinks. It still smells like my parents. I can smell my mother's perfume, my father's cigar smoke, and old stains of grape juice and cherry pie. I remember a time when I was young, when I could reach out the window and pluck a gooseberry from its bush, pop it in my mouth, and wheeze at its sourness. Arnez and I used to stage plays on the front porch of this house. Silly Western plays where I would be an Indian and he would be the cowboy, wrapping me up in a rope and play shooting me in the head.

"Do you want me to go get him?" she asks.

"No," I say. "No. It's okay. Go home. I'll get him and give him something to eat. Did he eat anything?"

"Granola," she says.

"Okay. See you tomorrow."

She has gone. I go upstairs to my father's locked door, carrying a plate of cheese and crackers. I tap at the door, the soft peck I remember from childhood as my mother woke us for church.

"Dad? Dad?" I unlatch the door, and it swings open. My father is on his bed, sitting upright. He is completely naked and is staring out the window. His legs are spread out and sweat rolls off them, turning the light blue sheets a darker shade. His penis hangs between his legs, and I am sure this is what killed my mother. Moments like this ate her alive. She would call me at 3 a.m. saying, "You know what he did, Teddy? Do you know? He went outside with no pants on to get the mail. Bill and Tammy Rae both saw him out there. They came over and brought him back inside. I answered the door to my naked husband and our friends. Can you imagine it, Teddy?" She'd go on, and I kept silent because I felt like she was dropping in on my life and had no right.

She should keep her stories to herself, I thought, but now I want to run to the phone and call Arnez.

My father is not completely gone. Occasionally, we can still watch a baseball game together. Even though he can no longer follow every play of the game, he can, sometimes, still keep up with the score. When I go into his room with the plate of Saltines and cheese, it is as if he snaps back to where he should be and notices his nakedness.

"Get out!" he shouts at me. "Get the hell out of here!" I drop the plate on his nightstand, close the door behind me, and slink down to the floor. I cry because when I went into the room, I wanted to tell him about the fake cowboy, and I wanted to ask him what I should do. Did he have any advice? Even if it meant staring into his eyes where nothing happened, it would have been enough to look at his face.

I wake up on the couch with the lights off. The clock's tick rings in the room. I think about Dad and remember that I had locked the door on my way out. His windows are nailed shut. He has probably torn the room apart again looking for the key. He probably urinated in the corner. Keeping him caged isn't what I ever had in mind. None of this is what I had in mind. I can still see the fake cowboy's hat, glowing in the sun like some demonic halo. I pick up the phone and call the IHOP.

A woman answers.

"Is Jenny there?"

"God no," the woman says. "She works days."

"Can I get her phone number?"

"Who is this?"

I hang up and wait most of the night watching reruns of M.A.S.H. and Charlie's Angels. I hit the remote OFF button and pick up an old book from the end table. There are stacks of books all over the house that my mother used

as decorations. I've never read any of them. This one is a
hunting guide. *How to Train Your Bird Dog.* I open it and read
the first section. *A good dog is a hunter's best asset. In order to
have the best possible dog, you must first train the dog to live in a pen.*
I put the book down, check the time. It's nearly five. I call
IHOP.

A man answers.

"Is Jenny there?" I ask.

"I'll check. She clocks in at five."

There is a clunk when he lays down the receiver. I can
hear him calling out for someone named Jeff, and I wonder
if that is the fake cowboy. I hear them talking, followed by a
woman's voice. The receiver clunks again. There is the sound
of flesh rubbing across the plastic.

"This is Jenny," she says.

I breathe in and then say, "Hi. My name is Ted. You were
my waitress the other day."

"Look," she says, "I'm sorry if you left too much for a
tip, okay? It's not my fault."

"Tip?"

"It happens," she says. "Get over it."

"Wait," I say. "This doesn't have anything to do with a
tip. I wanted to ask you a question."

"I've got a boyfriend," she says.

"No," I say, "that's not it. I wanted to ask about someone
who works there."

"Yeah?"

"Yes. The man with the cowboy hat."

"Who?"

There's a clang, a loud bash, and then cursing.

"Is everything all right?" I ask.

"Shit," she says. "Goddamnit, Terry. Get a fucking grip."
Her voice comes back onto the phone. "Who were you
talking about?"

"The man with the fake cowboy hat."

"Oh," she says. "Him? He's not gay."

"No," I say. "That's not it. I was wondering if he is dangerous."

"Dangerous?"

"Yes," I say. "Do you think he is dangerous?"

"I wouldn't fuck with him," she says. "Look, this is fascinating and all, but I've got to go. I'm on the clock now."

"Yeah," I stammer. "I'm sorry."

She hangs up. I hold the phone for a long time until I can feel the sweat in my palm. The air is cool, and upstairs I hear Dad moving around, getting ready to wake up. I think I should make some coffee, but I don't. I wait until I hear him try the door. Then I go up and let him out for the day.

Right after Dad's fortieth birthday, one celebrated in our backyard with much fanfare, lights, and even a Mexican hat dance, he decided to take me on a road trip to Kansas City. We were going to a car show, I remember, but why that particular show, I can't recall. We drove on Highway 50, the one that cuts across Missouri just below the major Interstate. Missouri unveils around the bends and curves. Little towns, bigger towns, and tractors on the roadside or buried deep in the fields of fescue grass, occasional corn.

Just outside of Kansas City we passed a trailer court with a clubhouse named South Fork after the *Dallas* ranch house, with streets designated "Bobby Drive" and "Sue Ellen Lane." It was enough to give us a chuckle. On the way back, I felt closer to him.

We stopped at a small bar in California, Missouri, for a few beers and a burger. I felt, up to that point, that I hadn't really known my father at all. When we were young, he spent much of his time at the retail store selling vacuum cleaners and washing machines. He worked over holidays and put in extraordinary amounts of overtime. I admired his hard-nosed work ethic now. But years ago, I found it elusive as well as odd that a man would want to be so detached from his family for so many months out of the year. Christmas was strange around our house, waking up with everyone gathered so close.

I bought the first round of beers and remarked at how wonderful the trip had been, how the car show had been truly amazing with so many different models and years. I knew nothing about cars, and, I believe, neither did my dad, but he nodded in agreement. He looked old in the dim light. I never remember thinking of him as old until that point. With the beer, light, and his balding head, he looked like something I could have pictured now; something I wished would never happen, but I knew it would. That's what getting old is, I suppose. Acknowledging it is only part of the pain, if there is anything involved with pain at all.

"You know," he said, "this has been fun. I haven't had this much fun in a while." He said it flat, as if it should be said.

"Yes," I said.

"Ted," he said, "have you ever been in a fight?"

I thought hard about this, paused, and said, "No. Not that I can think of." When I said it, I wanted to buy it back and bury it. It was the kind of thing you lied about when you were from a small town.

"It's not a bad thing," he said, after another sip of his beer. "It's not. Not really. I mean it doesn't make you less of a man." He drank again, more talkative now. "I mean, look at me. I'm not a fighter, not the least. I've been in a few in my time, I guess, but nothing like some other people. Don't ever be afraid of anything," he said. "You'll only end up tossed out on the street." When he told me that, I wondered if he had lost his job. I didn't ask.

The barmaid brought another pitcher of beer and set a bowl of peanuts on the table. She was tall and lean with hair stretching down like a frayed rope to save her ass from falling. Dad took her by the arm and pulled her down into the seat next to him. He winked at her, and she giggled. They talked and flirted for a while before she got up to leave. I don't remember what they talked about, but I knew it was something Dad wanted to say to a woman.

When she left, Dad turned back to me and said, "You sat there and said nothing. That's not the way to make it work," and went back to drinking. Later, when we left the bar, the sunlight hit and blinded us. It was hot, stifling, and his Dodge Duster had no air conditioning. All the way home, we rode with the windows down, wind yelling in our ears and making our faces cold and raw.

We are in IHOP again. It is around noon, and I blatantly refused to bring Dad in earlier because of the fake cowboy. He works mornings. Although Dad is thrown off a bit, it is still worth it, not seeing that guy. Dad rummages around on his plate, as if searching for the right food. He has been stirring his grits for the better part of an hour.

"Dad," I say, "why don't you eat your green beans? You like green beans." I always feel as if everyone is watching me when I say things like this.

"Beans, beans, the musical fruit," Dad begins singing. "The more you eat, the more you toot."

"All right," I say. "Let's just eat."

"The more you toot, the better you feel. Why not have beans for every meal?" The grits have fallen off his plate onto his pants. He looks down at them. "Damn beans," he says. "Arnez," he says, "who's that woman you're with? She looks like a Jew." He says this loud—loud enough for the people quietly enjoying their sandwiches, pancakes, and sausage to hear. "Being with a woman," he says, "is like taking out the trash. You always have to know when they are full." When things like this come up and he starts talking in ways that make no sense, I usually take him home. But today I'm tired. I don't feel like dragging him out of IHOP with him screaming in protest because he didn't get a short stack of pancakes. Today, I let him ramble on, which he does. When I think about it, it doesn't really matter what the fake cowboy says. No one would blame me in this nightmare.

I gather my books and books on tape and start shoving them in my shoulder bag. I've found this bag to be the most important item I own. I pack everything I could possibly need in it. I am never without the thing I need most, something for escape, salvation, or emergency: Band-Aids; toothpaste; vacation brochures; Dad's extra underwear; a fresh pair of socks; a clean, wrinkled shirt; duct tape; and a copy of *Catcher in the Rye*. If there is a situation, outside of a nuclear attack, I'm ready for it. I wonder if anyone has been so prepared for anything, and I look at my dad and think *No*.

"We're leaving?" he asks as I shoulder the leather bag.

"Soon," I say. He looks upset, but I know it's time to go, even if he is going to have one of his fits.

He doesn't though. He keeps his composure, and we walk out into the hot sun. I load him in the Jeep Cherokee, and we drive home, him constantly watching the road, pointing at places he thinks he knows, waving at people he believes know him.

"Dad," I say, knowing he won't look at me, "I'm sorry about the other day. I'm sorry I hit you." He doesn't say anything, just keeps waving out the window. He doesn't know he is waving at Marie Potts, a woman I used to have a thing for but never really involved myself with. She is putting a stack of flowers into the back of her car. Marie works for Aaron & Sons Mortuary. She is the florist, and I first met her at my Uncle Mack's funeral. She was arranging some daisies on the casket. They looked incredibly out of place, but my Aunt Ida had insisted. Marie was putting her best effort into making them look somber. Dad waves on, like a little kid, and we pull away from Marie and her flowers, head toward home where, I hope, Lotta will have something simmering on the stove for dinner. There's a twinge of hunger already coming on. For years now, I've felt as if I can't put enough in.

We sit out on the front porch, and there are fireflies in the air. Their little dots of light make trails across the evening—a path to follow. I can see where they are going, and I decide to catch them in a jar. It's easy work since they are so predictable, sort of like what I've become. "So, we'll see you next week," the workers say, and I say, "Same bat time, same bat channel," to try and add some spice to it, but it remains bland. Routine is a haven for Dad and a sanctuary for me—a place where I can hide. The fireflies are all bundled up, and I slap the jar's lid down, poke a few holes in its top with my rusted pocket knife, and hand it to Dad. He holds it close to his face; the little bugs toss light across his nose and eyes. He has, it seems, a true understanding of what is inside the jar, more so than I ever will. Sometimes I think his illness, despite its setbacks and annoyances for both of us, is really an eye opener. Alzheimer's makes him more aware of small things like the color of toothpaste, the shine of a doorknob, and the way these fireflies make light. That, in a way, is wonderful. But I know he is only looking at the blinking lights, the way tourists do in Vegas, the way they are overwhelmed by the excess.

"If you shake it gently," I say to him, leaning close, "they fly around. It's like disrupting their whole world." He smiles into the jar, and there is enough light to give off his reflection over the etched *Ball* logo.

"It's nice," he says before he drops the jar. It shatters at his feet. The glass falls on his white socks. The fireflies drift, buzzing around our heads for only a moment before they join the other random flashes. Early on, when I first took

Dad, a moment like this would have frightened me. I would have leapt up, frantically sweeping the glass with my hand, afraid he would step on it. Now I watch the fireflies and let the glass lie at our feet. If he cuts himself, I'll bandage it. I wonder when parents reach this stage of acceptance. When do they finally realize there is very little they can do to protect their children? I feel this way now. Even though I've never had kids, and probably never will, I know that sinking feeling a parent has when watching something tragic on television that has happened to another child somewhere. This is nothing new, I know now. It's not a special case, but for me it happened without the experience of raising anything.

I take Dad's hand and lead him on a short walk. We go out and down the walk, circle the lawn, and frighten the fireflies. The sun is down, but it is still casting its orange haze over the Western horizon. I can see the outlines of trees in the distance, the other houses where lights are starting to come on, where it might be board game night, meatloaf night, or watch-television-till-we-drop night. Whatever. Tonight is walk night for us, and Dad's hand is on my arm. I'm leading him down the sidewalk, careful to watch for cracks or raised sections where he might trip. He stares straight ahead. His eyes are glassy and watery, as if he is about to cry.

"I met a man," I tell him, "in the park the other day, and he said he wanted money because he saw me hit you." Dad turns to me, his eyes the same. "What should I do?" I ask.

"You should pay him," my father says. "Always pay what you owe."

Dad is in his wheelchair. He is so tired. He can't walk because he tossed and turned all night, calling out to a great-grandmother I never knew. He is in pain, I know. I can feel it myself, and I wonder if he knows I know about the pain. I slip two Tylenol between his thin, pale lips. He spits them out. They shine like little jewels on the navy blue rug.

"Do you want to go to IHOP?" I ask in a loud voice. I yell it to wake him up. He does, so he nods. "Pancakes?" I ask again, just to be sure. He nods again.

We pull into the parking lot. I'm hoping the fake cowboy works on Fridays. I have three thousand dollars in my back pocket. It is almost everything I have. There is enough left to pay the house payment next month and to keep the lights on, but beyond that, I don't know. I will ask my boss, Fred, for an advance. I will tell him the whole story, leaving out certain parts, and I hope the three thousand is enough for now. Dad can't go to a nursing home, not one where he would have to go because I couldn't afford better and Arnez won't pay. He is always complaining about not having any money anyway. These pictures of Dad strapped to a bed keep going through my mind as I open the heavy glass IHOP doors with *Open 24-7* painted on the outside.

Even though this is out of routine for Dad, it seems important to do something with him because Lotta quit the week before. Since then, I haven't known what to do. I've been playing checkers with him for the past week; me making all the moves. He has been anxious ever since she left. Her brown face and meaty arms must have comforted him in some way, maybe reminded him of his mother. I pull him out, plop him in the wheelchair, and we roll across the parking lot. I inspect the cars, hoping to find some sign of the fake cowboy's car, even though I have no idea what it looks like, what model it is, or anything. Maybe, I think, he leaves that hat in the car while he works.

It is 4:30 a.m. This IHOP is the only one open this early. It is near the highway, and the truckers will be pulling in soon from an overnight run. The inside smells like freshly brewed coffee and a grease explosion. There are sizzling sounds coming from behind the long counter that separate the restaurant from the kitchen. An old man sits smoking a cigar three booths down from the door. He has gray hair and is holding a fedora hat. He is wearing a jacket. It's not that cold, but it is cool enough for an old man to wear a jacket. Dad and I take our usual table. The waitress, Samantha, comes around. She's a nice girl, cute for the most part, a girl I might call my type if I had the time to evaluate types. Samantha has these little fingers like the tips of quill pens. She writes swiftly in short hand, replying in her mid-range voice—nothing you would hear in a choir. When she says, "Is that it?" it makes you want to order more. I add a side of bacon to my order. For a minute, Dad and I are alone, watching out the window where the dew collects on the patchwork grass. The streets are slick. A cab drives by. Its lights are off. Dad watches all of this, not registering any of it to my knowledge. It is the little stuff, I think, that you must miss. Those tiny, insufficient things like the sound of a car on wet streets that eats the brain away.

"Dad," I say. "Dad? Do you see the streets? They are like a mirror this morning. Dad, the end of the world will be something to see."

When our order comes, it is not Samantha who brings it. Instead, it is a tall man in an apron, who I know—without looking—is the fake cowboy. He sets the orders in front of us and sits down next to me.

"I'm on my break," he says. "Mind if I pass it with you folks?"

I'm a little queasy, thinking about the money. "No," I say. "We don't mind." Dad gives a little nod as if he is in on the conversation.

"Looks like you've got quite an appetite there," fake cowboy says. "Why don't you share a little of the wealth." He reaches over and takes a slice of my extra bacon. I hadn't really wanted it anyway, so I let him reach and reach again until the bacon is gone. I reach into my pocket and pull the money out. I lay it on the table so he can see.

"It's all I have," I say. "It's everything."

"It's not everything," the fake cowboy says. "There's lots left, I'm sure." He smiles at me. His teeth are straight and colored yellow around the edges. "You know the difference between people like me and people like you? I take what is right in front of me. I see an opportunity, and I take it. I won't settle for second best. This," he waves his hand around, "is all a big fucking dodge. There is nothing for a person like me here. I take chances. I make things happen."

He goes for my coffee and the money. Dad reaches out and slaps his hand, hard, a resounding smack of smooth flesh on flesh. The fake cowboy pulls back.

"What the hell?"

"Shut up," Dad says. "Stop stealing from your brother."

The fake cowboy rubs his hand and says, "What the fuck?"

Samantha comes around with a pot of coffee. She refills the cups all around. "Do you know these guys, Terry?" she asks, and the fake cowboy nods, slightly.

"I oughta knock the shit out of you," he says after Samantha leaves.

"Shut up," Dad yells. "Shut up. Both of you."

The manager leaves the kitchen and cranes his neck down the aisle at us. Dad is still yelling. "Shut up. Shut up. Shut up. I'll whip the both of you."

"Calm down," I tell Dad and hand him his coffee cup. I turn to the fake cowboy, "Please," I say, "he doesn't know what he is saying." The manager is at our table now.

"What's going on? Terry, do you know these people?" He looks at Dad, at the money, at me. "Do you know him?"

"Sort of," I say.

"Terry, why don't you take your break someplace else."

The fake cowboy stands up, stares at Dad, and walks away, still staring and rubbing his attacked hand.

"Look," the manager says to me, "don't get Terry wound up. If he gives you any more trouble, you let me know. Okay? I'll handle it. I'll call the son-of-a-bitch's parole officer." He says this as he is following Terry down the row of booths, quickening his step, telling Samantha to bring more coffee and a free doughnut.

Dad's eyes are as wet as the streets, and he is looking at me again the same way he did in the bar in California, Missouri. With those eyes, he is telling me it's all right.

Even This Is Silence

The boy's mother had come back. Henry buckled the boy in the backseat as Alice situated herself up front. Henry and Alice had cared for the boy, their nephew, since his mother had run off to Montana with a vacuum salesman a year ago. Over the phone, she had said she felt refreshed, as if she were ready to have a son again, ready to take on a new life, and that the married man who lived two blocks away and had a son of his own had come back.

"We've both," she said, "dipped ourselves in the spiritual well of forgiveness and love."

They could still trace the moon's outline as they drove south out of St. Louis. The Buick's wheel bearings hummed. Around the moon hung a mist, and the boy drew circles around it in the condensation that formed on the backseat window. Alice knitted on a pair of socks for the boy's mother.

"I've always admired her," she said about her sister. "I've always wondered how she managed after Hurston died. She was always able." Alice stared out where the headlights fell on the highway. Ahead of them, red taillights floated in the early morning cold.

"She's back now," Henry said. "I guess that means something."

"It does," Alice answered. "It means a lot."

In the backseat, the boy drew circles on the window and watched them disappear.

The Buick slumped into Wynott around 9 a.m. Henry saw it as a lost tourist would: hollow buildings; cow shit dotting the highway; cold, blank, and rusted-out trucks sunk in dried mud and weeds. Three crows pecked at a smashed carcass. Quiet oozed like sap from the maple trees.

They drove past the park and the town lake, which was more of a pond, and past the feed store onto Main Street—a long, narrow strip of buildings with fake fronts and boards nailed across the weak-looking doors. Main took them past the short City Hall with its American flag, the Dairy Freeze, and the two-story First Methodist Church that faced the Second Baptist Church. Gravel parking lots. Rows of blackberry bushes hemmed in by short fences, and clapboard houses—some leaning, with short porches and storm doors made pointless by holes in the screen. Henry slowed as the road curved right and up a small hill to the school, which was surrounded by oaks, maples, and a few strategically placed blooming dogwoods. A little green sprinkled the maples and oaks with life. Dust blew from where kids had trampled the grass. They turned right and drove a block to the old house where Alice had grown up, where her sister had returned. The dried up house was a memory.

When Henry slammed the station wagon's door, he saw Beth come out on the porch wearing a sundress that flitted around her legs. The sight of her took him back to 1965: picking up Alice for a date and watching her sister dangle long legs off the porch swing—her thin, white ankles and long calves exposed. He blushed and opened the back door. Beth ran to the boy.

"My little man," she said into his hair. "How I've missed my little man." Then, to Henry, she said, "Thank you. Thank you. Thank you. You are God's gift."

Henry blushed again, and they went inside where the smell of mothballs made him nauseous. In the parlor, he sat in the same seat where he had waited for Alice, where Beth had flirted with him. He thought of Hurston's accident and how he could have had his face crushed beyond recognition if he had stayed and taken the factory job like his father had wanted.

A vase of sunflowers and daisies stood on the end table, dried crisp by time. Around the table lay dust and little scraps of flowers. With only the shaded light coming through the window, the flowers were dull brown and black.

They all sat down. The dust plumed around them, hovering in the air. Henry swiped it away. It waved in front of him, moving away from his hand and closing back. It hung in the light.

Beth brought out some hot raspberry tea and gave them all a mug, even the boy, who sat cross-legged on the floor.

"How was your trip?" Alice asked.

"Oh, it was much more than a trip," Beth said. "A trip you take to the Grand Canyon or Mt. Rushmore. No, this wasn't a trip, Allie, this was an experience."

"How was your experience then?"

"It was grand, Allie, just grand. It made me realize exactly who I'm supposed to be."

"Who is that?" Henry asked.

"I'm supposed to be me," she said. "Just who I am. I'm supposed to grow, bloom, wilt, and die."

They sat in the parlor and drank their raspberry tea, watching the sun go down. Wynott stretched into a ribbon of light, a crease in Baker County turned over as if into a grave. Henry wondered where the boy fit into the growing, blooming, wilting, and dying.

Alice said, "That's wonderful, Elizabeth. It sounds like you've really made a go for yourself."

"I did," Beth said. "I've made a heck of a go. He and I both said it was the best thing we've ever done." Her head went down, her eyes on the floor. "For ourselves, I mean," she said.

"It must be," Alice said through her tea's steam. "You look better than ever. You're absolutely glowing."

On the floor, the boy began fidgeting. He took his mug and placed it on the end table near the flower vase.

"Not there," Alice said. "Don't put it there. It'll make a stain."

The boy took the cup back, leaving a clear ring in the dust where the shiny wood shone through. *Did it matter*, Henry thought, *here with all this dust? Do stains matter?* He kept his mouth shut and drank his tea, the way he always had, while Alice and her sister spoke.

"I think we all need some dinner," Beth said.

Henry stayed in the round-backed chair that scrunched his shoulders as the two sisters entered the kitchen. He could envision Alice's father sitting across the room, the old man's face hidden behind pipe smoke. The man had never said a word to Henry, not one, except after Henry and Alice were married when he had said, "You don't deserve any of this."

The old man knew about Henry and Alice and about Henry and Beth. Henry felt small in the room. From the kitchen, he heard Beth saying, "You should see Montana, Allie. It has these wide skies like nothing you've ever seen before. Nothing to block your view. You'd think you could see all the way to the ocean, but you can't. You really can't see that far at all. It just *feels* like the whole place swallows you up."

Light from down the hall came into their room in a thin line. It slipped across the carpet, up the bedside, onto his face where his eyes were open, watching the door. He could hear her down the hall, cooing at the boy.

"My angel," she said. "My little man-angel."

Henry turned over. Alice snored in broken snorts. Outside, the moon painted the yard a pale blue. He thought if he breathed out, fog would form in front of his face, but it wasn't that cold. He got out of bed and went to the window, looked out across the lawn to the street and then at the town of sparse lights. He could see the high school where he and Tom Sullis had thrown rocks through a teacher's window. Beyond that were the water tower and the road to his parents' old house, which still stood, which he still owned and paid taxes on and never visited. He could trace the road that led west out of town toward the wide fields and random, back-country roads where he had spent most of his youth. Back there, just beyond the tree line, was where he had first kissed a girl, first gotten laid, and first drunk moonshine from a still. All of these things he remembered. But he remembered his time with Alice the most, and more than that his time with Beth and how the moon looked on her face. Alice snorted. Henry went out into the dark hallway, his feet pressing against the cool boards.

The floor made noises as loud as cracks opening in the earth. Sometimes he dreamt about just that—the ground opening up beneath him. He would walk along the crack; beneath his feet was nothing, but he wouldn't fall. He would only watch it grow and expand until it became all he could see. Moon shadows moved over the white paint. He could see her, sprawled across the bed with the boy next to her, cradled in her arm.

He watched them for a half an hour or more, their stomachs falling almost in unison. Then he crept back to his room. He stretched out in the bed and listened for passing cars—a sound he had become used to in the city, but he heard nothing but the house's creaks and snaps as its sixty-year-old wooden beams bent in the wind and Alice's snore, which was softer now.

1968. His father's Ford trolled up Allegheny Hill, just past the city limits, with Beth nestled beside him, her arm around his neck, and a sweet honey scent of her blowing through the car as they came up around a bend to the hill's crest where the trees dropped off and, as if out of the forest's mouth, a meadow spilled. They could see the parked cars in the moonlight, dark beasts with fogged windows. He found a spot, one a few yards from a car he knew—another guy on the football team. He parked, turned the engine off, and let the car wheeze out its last breath.

"What do you want?" Beth had said. He had kissed her on the neck, on the shoulder, and down her front until she put her arms around him. Out the Ford's front window, he could see Wynott, the little lights like fingers pointing.

They had necked for a while and made love in the backseat. Then Beth had her legs up on the dashboard. A cigarette dangled from her mouth. The car was black and quiet, aside from the soft noises their bare skin made on the vinyl seats. He took her hand and put it on his leg.

"There's a whole world out there," he said. "What are you going to do?"

She hadn't said anything for a while. She had let the air around them lay still, stinking of her cigarette smoke.

"I'm going to stay right here," she said. "I'm going to make a go of it. It's not so bad. Look at it," and she moved her hand from his leg and motioned out the window. Below, people began turning out their porch lights. They could see the outlines of treetops at the meadow's edge. The streetlights still glowed—their hollow light laid out in perfect and punctual rows.

"I'll stay with you," he said.

"What about Alice?"

They rarely talked about her sister. Her name made both of them shiver when they said it in the Ford on Allegheny Hill.

"I suppose I'll tell her," he said.

"I suppose we should tell her."

Henry looked over at her. There had never been a "we" before.

"How should we do it?"

"We should be flawless," she said. "There can't be any mistakes."

The windshield had fogged while they talked. He leaned forward and wiped it clean so they could see the stars. Out in the dark, the other cars all sat facing the town, as if answering to it, with their windshields all fogged up. This was their last night together, although he didn't know it at the time. As he thought about it, if he had known, he would have said more. He would have told Alice. He would have waited longer until the answers to those questions behind everyone's eyes had run out.

Henry pulled himself out of bed in the morning and went downstairs where Alice and Beth had pancakes on the table. The boy sat and ate while the two sisters drank coffee. Henry took a vacant chair. He piled some pancakes on his plate.

"Did you sleep well?" Beth asked.

He told her he did.

Beth had gone away before. First to college and then to California, but she always came back. When she left for California, Henry married Alice on a Wednesday at the courthouse in Harriston. They had moved two months later to St. Louis. Henry told himself he hadn't waited. He wasn't the type to wait anymore or to keep quiet anymore. He was going to say things. He had said things. He had told Alice about how he had taken her sister out when they were younger. He hadn't told her everything.

The boy wanted to do something. Henry took him out the back door, across a small, open field to where the creek ran across the back of Beth's property. It ran shallow, low enough to see the tadpoles' eyes. The boy squatted and watched the little swimmers dart beneath the water. Henry leaned near him on a rock.

"They are baby frogs," he said.

"Who?"

"Those things. Those are baby frogs."

"They don't look like frogs," the boy said.

"No," Henry said, "but someday they will. You don't look like you used to either."

"I guess not," the boy said.

Henry went over to him. "They make great fishing bait if you can catch one, but usually, you need to buy them."

"Why?"

"Because they are fast. They slide right through your fingers."

"I can catch one," the boy said.

"Go on and try."

He leaned down, hunched on his knees, and put his hands near the water. Then he grabbed with his fist, and the water splashed onto Henry's trousers.

"I've got him," the boy said, waving his closed fist in the air. "I've got him right here."

He opened his hand and found it empty.

"It's all right," Henry said. "It's not easy to catch one, you know."

"Have you ever caught one?" the boy asked.

"Yes," Henry said. "Once or twice."

They knelt together in the clumped fescue grass, a breeze on them, and the strong odor of cow dung in the air. Henry took Earl's hands and put them down in the water.

"Hold them still now," Henry said, lifting his own hands up and watching the boy's shimmer and dance in the sunlight beneath the water.

Still. Crickets. The sound of water rolling over rocks. A dragonfly floated down, landed on the boy's shoulder, and rested. Its wings moved with the breeze.

Eventually, the boy learned to reach beneath the tadpole with both hands, bring his hands together to form a sort of cup, and raise it slowly. Then the boy had one in his hands. It swam and flipped. He put his nose close and smelled it.

"The idea," Henry told him, "is not to disrupt their existence. If you do that, you'll never catch one."

"Thanks," the boy said. "Were you ever any good at this?"

"I've never been much good to anyone," Henry said as he brushed the dirt off his knees. He reached down and picked a stone out of the creek and stared into its glossy surface. The slime made it slip through his fingers as he turned it over and over. He tossed it into the creek and could see it sink to the bottom. He said, "I guess I'm sorry for that."

They drove around town. Henry showed Earl the streets where he used to ride his bike and the houses where his friends used to live. He told stories. The boy listened and stared out the window at the passing houses, set back off the street with long front lawns and carports instead of garages. The boy didn't remember much about living in Wynott. He had only been here a few years; they were his young years—times he couldn't remember.

"I played in the backyard," he told Henry. "I went to the creek once and made Mama mad."

Henry took Earl to Dan's Dairy Freeze and bought

chocolate malts. Dan Herman was there. He recognized Henry and said hello, a little shock in his face. They sat in the cracked vinyl booth and drank their malts.

"Do you like it here, Earl?" Henry asked.

"I guess," the boy said. His mouth looked small on the straw. His cheeks pulled in as he drank.

Then, without thinking, Henry began telling the boy other stories. He began telling him about the boy's mother and how beautiful she was earlier in her life. He told Earl about picking her up on Saturdays and taking her up to the field on Allegheny Hill, about sneaking her out the back while Alice sat in the front room with her father, both of them reading newspapers. Around him, the people kept their voices low, mumbled through their cheeseburgers. Their eyes stayed down. Dan Herman stood behind the counter, wiping it down with a soft rag. He looked away as Henry spoke.

"I never thought she would leave me," Henry said.

Earl took both drinks and threw them away. When he came back, he sat next to Henry.

"Mama gets away a lot," he said.

"She does," Henry said. "She leaves. That's what she does."

A few people came in and sat near them. They chewed on hamburgers and fries, and some of them recognized Henry's face, even with the lines in his brow and around his mouth. Henry could sense them staring at him. He began to twitch in his seat, the vinyl popping and cracking under him.

"Are you ready to go?" he asked Earl. The boy nodded, and they left Dan's Dairy Freeze and got back into Henry's Buick. There were no clouds in the sky. The sun was bright and made the dashboard hot.

"I haven't been back here in nine years," Henry said.

On Main Street, Henry turned his eyes from oncoming cars. He focused past them, toward the house where he could collect Alice and drive back to St. Louis where no one knew him, where people's voices were loud, where you could say things and no one would notice.

Alice and Beth sat on the back porch with the sun on their faces. Beth had on a light dress. It flapped around her bony shoulders. Her plumper sister wore a dark navy skirt and blouse. As she sweated through it, she fanned herself with a newspaper.

"My God," Alice said, "where have you been? I've been looking for you."

Earl went over to the railing and stood looking across the field to the creek.

"We went for a drive," Henry explained. "Stopped for a malt."

"At the Dairy Freeze?"

"Yes," Henry said.

"We're going to stay awhile," Alice told him. "I'm going to make sure my baby sister gets settled in."

Beth stood up and came over to Henry.

"I'm going to be all right," she said. "I just need some urging."

Henry said nothing as Beth went past him into the house.

"I don't know," Henry said. He rubbed his chin, a signal to his wife that he disapproved, one she only sometimes acknowledged.

"It's the thing to do," Alice said. "Like old times."

"Old times," Henry said. He turned to look out the window at his Buick parked at the curb. The tires were low on the back. He would have to have them replaced and that meant taking the car to the Collins Lube and Tire where people had known and liked his father but had never known him in the same way.

"Yes," Alice said. "Old times. Maybe we could take a drive in the country someday. It's been so long since I've seen the country. I could just drink it all in."

"That would be nice," Beth said. "We could all go. The four of us."

"Look," Earl pointed, "look, look."

They could see the rain as it fell in swaths. It advanced across the field, an army of bullet-like drops, shooting into the ground. Henry took Alice and pulled her up, grabbed the boy, and pushed them both inside as the rain marched over the back lawn, up the porch steps, and finally onto the house. It moved so slowly they could follow its eastward movement across town. The line between the storm and sunlight was as clear as a tattoo on the earth.

"I've never," Alice said under her breath. She drank another glass of hot tea and went upstairs to lie down. The boy leaned against the front window, watching the storm as it engulfed Wynott—first the school, then downtown, then the east side where the railroad tracks ran, and finally the saw mill. Mountains of sawdust turned dark brown under the rain's weight.

"How cool," the boy said.

"It's pretty cool," Henry told him. "It moves so slowly because the air is so heavy the wind can't blow it very fast."

"It disrupted our whole world," Earl said, still watching the storm, not looking at Henry.

Beth was in the kitchen fixing sandwiches. Henry went in and saw her in her dry dress, how it hung limply around her legs as dresses always had on her. He wanted to take her hand, to kiss her, to do something that would make sense. At that moment, nothing made sense, not the rain, not the boy, not how he had left. Beth stood there looking at him.

"I know why you left," he said to her.

"Yes," she said, "you do."

"What about the boy?" he asked her. He wondered if his eyes did the same to her that Dan Herman's did to him.

"He'll stay," she said. "He'll make it."

Outside, thunder and lightning began, and the

houselights dimmed. From the living room, they heard Earl cry out, "Awesome."

"He's a good kid," Henry said. "I hope he doesn't end up as fucked up as us."

"He will," she said. "It's the nature of things. It's the nature of this place."

"Why can't we ever talk?" Henry said, exasperated. "Why can't we ever just say things that we should say?"

"That's not in the nature of this place," she said. She put the sandwiches down, and he took one and bit into it. It tasted salty, and the sharp mustard stung his tongue.

"I swore I wouldn't come back here," he told her, wiping the mustard off his lips. "I swore when you left again that I wouldn't ever come back. I wouldn't look at any of these people again."

Thunder rocked the house again, and the lights went out. Beth sat down at the table and lit a candle.

"I swore it, too," she said. "So here we are."

Little rain droplets gathered just inside the open kitchen window. When the breeze blew in, it carried with it the smell of wet wildflowers. 1963. It had been raining; the back porch soaked straight through until the planks bled out underneath and began to bow. It had rained for four days straight, and the ground felt like a marsh everywhere. On the only dry place, the sidewalk, he crushed wiggling earthworms and slugs with his shoes. They couldn't be avoided. They were like pebbles scattered across a driveway. He told Alice the day before that they would drive over to Harriston, come hell or high water, to see a movie. Beth came along, for the first time, and he remembered watching her through the rearview, how she kept looking up at him with her young eyes, fifteen then, and her small smile. *And here it is*, he thought, standing in front of her now with the sun coming through the window behind her and with sandwiches laid out like stacks of cards. He heard the boy in the next room. He stood at the front door watching the rain move on toward the east.

Beth said, "You don't have to stay. You can go. All of you can." She chopped a cucumber in two. "Take Earl," she said.

"We can't do that," Henry said. "Look," he said, "I'm not the kind of person who can barge in and take over a situation. That's not what I do. I just fall into things."

He went out to where the boy stood on the front porch. They could barely see the rain line now. Alice came downstairs, out onto the porch.

"I guess that's about it," she said, shielding her eyes and watching the rain cloud.

"We can stay," he said. "We can stay because I don't know what else to do."

"Of course we can," Alice said. "It's like old times."

"I may go back," Henry said.

She looked over at him. He turned to her and saw her eyes. Their blue seemed deeper in the soft air after the rain. They were the same. It was all the same. The boy came down the steps.

"Aunty Alice says you're staying," he said.

Henry got into his Buick. The doors creaked. He turned the key and drove the car down to Collins Lube and Tire where he parked in front of the office and went inside. Joe Collins stood behind the counter, ruffling a newspaper. Henry tossed his keys on the counter.

"I'll be," Joe said.

"Hello, Joe," Henry said. "I need an oil change and two new back tires."

Joe Collins took the keys. He didn't say anything. He hung the keys on the rack behind the counter with all the other keys belonging to other cars of people who lived in Wynott. Henry thought about all those cars sunk in the mud, with weeds grown up around their windows, hiding the insides like fog.

RYAN STONE earned his MFA in fiction from the University of Missouri-St. Louis in 2004. He has served as the Editor for *Natural Bridge: A Journal of Contemporary Literature* and the Managing Editor/Fiction Editor for *River Styx*. He has taught writing for St. Louis Community College, Lewis and Clark Community College, The St. Louis Writers Workshop, Missouri State University-West Plains, and Drury University, and is currently a tenured member of the English Department at Danville Area Community College, Danville, IL where he teaches composition, creative writing, and literature. His fiction has appeared in numerous publications, including *The South Carolina Review*, *The Madison Review*, *Whiskey Island Magazine*, *Wisconsin Review*, *REAL: Regarding Arts and Letters*, and many others.

ANDREW KUFAHL is an aspiring professional photographer from Wisconsin. He currently spends much of his time improving his techniques in portraiture, nature, and still-life photography.

He says of his cover photo for *Best Road Yet*, "I was sitting in my car on my lunch break, fiddling with my iPhone. I had taken a couple of photos of my keys in the ignition and liked how the high-noon sun was illuminating the metal. I kept moving my iPhone around to different angles and accidentally got some sun flare in the top corner. When I reviewed the photo, I thought the sunburst was a cool effect, so I tried a few slightly different variations and angles to get more sunburst effects until I had one that I really liked."

See more of Andrew's work at www.flickr.com/photos/arkufahl

www.ingramcontent.com/pod-product-compliance
Lightning Source LLC
Chambersburg PA
CBHW020636250626
47154CB00008B/2710